THE MONSTER'S LOVER

First edition. January 22, 2019.

Written by Samantha MacLeod.

To Peter.

Don't read it.

FAIR WARNING

Welcome, reader!

I'm delighted you've chosen to spend time with Sol and Fenris in the dark shadows of the Ironwood forest.

Before we begin, let me issue a note of warning. This story contains graphic depictions of sexual encounters, violence, and attempted sexual assault. Like the Norse myths themselves, the Fenris Series is far from tame.

Also, *The Monster's Lover* is the first book in a five book series. While it can certainly be read and enjoyed as a standalone story, please be aware that this book is not the end. The next installment in Sol's story, *The Monster's Wife*, will come out in February of 2019. For a full schedule of release dates, please click here[1].

Still interested?

Then, dear reader, please do join me. The Ironwood Forest is waiting.

---

1. https://sammacleod.wordpress.com/2019/01/04/coming-soon-the-fenris-series/

CHAPTER ONE

"I don't want to go," I said.

Ma didn't even look up from the bread dough she was stretching across our flour-dusted tabletop. The basket of eggs sat next to the open door, heavy and demanding in the cold light of early morning.

"Sol," she said. "You have to go."

I bit my lip. My vision swam with tears already, but I couldn't let them spill down my cheeks. "Can't Egren take them?"

She sighed and her head dropped. "He's gone to the forest with Jael."

I should have gone to the forest instead. I should have gone anywhere else instead. I took a deep breath.

"The last time I went to town, Ma—"

"Don't." She turned. The dark circles under her eyes were like bruises on her thin, pale face.

"Ma, Maddie Liefsen spat on me. She spat in my face!"

"Ignore her. You'll be far enough away from the likes of them soon."

I shuddered as I thought of where exactly I'd be going. I'd always imagined Maddie Liefsen was a friend, the same way I supposed I'd imagined all the people in town were my friends. Before I'd been claimed by King Nøkkyn. I shifted in the doorway, hesitating. Perhaps, I could escape by offering to weed the potatoes instead.

"Sol. This is the last of the flour, and I still have four mouths to feed."

Anger flared inside me, hot and sudden. "I know!" I snapped. "At least until you sell me off!"

Ma's shoulders sank. I'd seen that gesture enough to last a lifetime in the months since Da died. My stomach knotted.

"Sorry," I mumbled.

Ma wiped her eyes with the back of her hand, leaving a streak of flour across the concave well of her cheek. "Just take the damn eggs. Go to Johmaersen. He'll trade you for flour."

She stood and dragged her leg across the floor. A logging accident had ruined her leg before I was born. Da used to say she worked as hard as a man in the woods. She'd been his partner, finding the rare purple oaks we owed the king.

I frowned as she wrapped her hands around the egg basket. Her busted leg was the reason I wasn't allowed to help in the forest, as if her injury proved all women were somehow incompetent, unable to handle the work of harvesting purple oaks, even though I was just as strong as my younger brother.

Ma's busted leg and my own thrice-damned face.

"I'll take it," I snapped before Ma could pick up the eggs and hobble toward me.

I grabbed the basket and stormed out, not waiting for her reaction, and not stopping until I'd reached the shade of our farthest apple tree. The fruits that had been so hard and tiny a month ago were now plump, showing the first blushes of red. In another few weeks, they'd be crisp and juicy, ready to harvest.

Another few weeks after that, and it would be time for me to leave.

I balanced the eggs against my hip, shading my eyes as I scanned the edge of the forest one last time. Not that I honestly expected my brothers to return now. They must have left this morning, while I was doing the washing in the river. It could be weeks before they return.

Or, they might never return.

My heart gave a funny little pang. Logging the Ironwood was dangerous, far too dangerous for two boys. Jael was nearly fully grown, but Egren was still a child. He said he wasn't afraid, but when I thought of him climbing into the dark canopy with a cold, sharp saw tucked under his arm, my chest tightened until I felt I couldn't breathe.

I would be far away soon, just like Ma said. I wondered if that would make me feel any better.

TOWN WAS HALF A DAY'S walk away. I'd be coming back in the dark, but the moon was nearly full, and I didn't fear the Ironwood forest. At least, I didn't fear the Ironwood more than was necessary. Once, I'd told Da I was afraid of the Fenris-wolf, the legendary monster haunting our forest. He'd laughed and laughed as he held me close to his chest.

"Is that a bad way to go, my beauty?" he asked. "When you could languish in illness, or suffer on the birthing bed? A quick death's the best any of us can ask of the Nine Realms."

A fresh round of tears threatened to obscure the trail to town. I blinked them back. He got his wish, my beloved Da. Jael had come back early from their logging expedition last winter, dragging the huge sled by himself, with Da's broken body laid out on it, cold and empty, his stiff, blue limbs filling the space where purple oak logs should have been stacked.

The wind blew up suddenly, Jael told us, his voice ragged and wounded. Da was in the treetop, cutting off branches for Jael to gather. The limb he'd stood upon had snapped with a dry crack like a flash of heat lightning, and Da had plunged to the forest floor. Jael said his back was broken instantly, leaving his wide-open eyes empty.

I realized in the bitter months after his death that he'd been right. Da'd had it easy with his quick exit. The rest of us had a quota to fill.

Jael couldn't finish harvesting the purple oak by himself, not even with little Egren's help. Last year's sudden, early frost had cost us most of our crops. We'd sold the cows first, then the pigs. Egren cried when our neighbor, Attin, led the pigs away, mourning the loss of all that smoked ham and bacon. Ma pressed her lips together and smiled as Attin counted out the coin, although I knew it was less than half of what she'd expected. And far less than what was fair.

"We'll have beans and potatoes for the winter," she'd insisted that night, as we laid out our coins on the table.

We'd counted and re-counted the money, my brothers and I. No matter how we arranged the dull, gleaming piles of chipped metal coins, it wasn't enough to make up for falling short on our lumber quota. We might have food for the winter, but food wasn't enough. This was a holding on King Nøkkyn's land, and we were obligated to provide His Highness with twenty cords of purple oak every year. Anything over twenty cords he would purchase, although he usually paid less than what we could charge to anyone else.

Of course, none of our other potential buyers controlled an army.

"What else can we offer Nøkkyn?" Jael asked. It was late at night; Egren was already curled in sleep in front of the fading embers of the fire. "What more would the king accept?"

Ma and Jael both turned to me, but it was several long minutes before I grasped their meaning.

Indeed, perhaps I did not fully grasp it until a turn of the moon later when Ma had dressed me in the soft green dress she kept in her chest and painted my lips and cheeks with bloodberries. Ma had altered the dress until the neckline plunged almost to my navel, exposing the full curve of my breasts. She'd kissed my reddened cheeks and told me to be strong.

King Nøkkyn's taxman had entered our home that spring to find me, dressed and painted, in front of the cool hearth. He was a thin, unpleasant man with a face like a fish's belly. He poked and prodded me, his dark eyes watching me much as the townsmen had inspected our dairy cow. I followed my mother's advice and did not meet his eyes although, when he pried open my mouth to examine my teeth, I had to fight the urge to bite him. When he'd left without writing Ma's name in his tax roster, I'd dared to hope that was the end of it.

But King Nøkkyn, the Mountain King himself, had come a fortnight later, riding a great black stallion and accompanied by his fish-faced taxman. Nøkkyn was a massive man with dark eyes, thin lips, and a severe nose. His horse trampled our smoothly swept dooryard with silver-shod hooves. Ma rushed me inside, stripping my everyday dress, pulling the smooth green one over my arms, and lacing up my back. She pinched my cheeks as the door creaked open.

Nøkkyn entered our home as if he owned it. And I supposed he did. He owned the Ironwood forest, after all, and everything in the forest.

"This is an expensive claim," Nøkkyn declared. His sharp eyes followed the exposed swell of my breasts. "Not even the Æsir of Asgard dare to travel so far into the Ironwood forest. It costs much to have my soldiers protect your holding here."

I bit my lip. No soldiers ever came this far. The only sign of King Nøkkyn's rule we ever saw was the great wagons which came once a year, collecting the purple oaks we'd harvested as our tithe and dragging them to town to load the great barges traveling down the Körmt river.

Nøkkyn turned to my mother the way a man would turn to a stray dog. "You and your husband were slaves, no?"

She nodded, her eyes on the floor.

Nøkkyn clucked deep in his throat. "To think my predecessor gave slaves such a holding… Well, it's not cheap to watch over this family. And here I understand you haven't fulfilled your quota for the year."

"Your Highness," Ma said, her wan voice trembling, "we do have other goods to exchange."

The King turned to me again. I didn't care for the flash that lit his eyes as he examined my nearly-bare chest. He took a step closer to me. His head almost brushed the rafters.

"Yes," he muttered. "I see."

He grabbed my breast through the green dress and pinched my nipple hard enough to make me flinch. I bit my tongue to keep from crying out and fought the urge to push his hand away.

I was goods, after all. Goods to exchange.

Nøkkyn's hand moved higher, sinking into my hair. With a yank, he pulled my head back. Then he leaned toward me until I could smell the sour tang of his sweat. He took a deep breath as he tugged on my hair, and the cold brass of his brooch pressed into the bare skin of my stomach. My skin crawled beneath his touch. He released me suddenly and shoved me backward. I staggered, hitting the stone of our hearth with my hip. Nøkkyn wiped his palm on his black cloak as though he'd just handled something dirty.

"She'll do," he said, speaking to no one in particular. "For this year, I suppose."

He left without a backward glance. Ma scurried after him. I heard the stomp of his great horse beyond our door.

"We'll collect her once the harvest is complete," his taxman said. His thin, reedy voice carried through the open door. "At the Reaping."

I shivered at his use of the old name for the Harvest Festival. Even the wealthiest families in town didn't call it the Reaping, as though the bad luck chained to that old name might follow them back to their secure brick houses, draining their wealth and happiness like light fading from the winter sky.

Nøkkyn's black horse deposited an enormous, steaming pile of shit on top of the basil patch in our kitchen garden before turning back to the village, and the men left without another word. It was mid-summer, and I was claimed.

Not as a wife, of course. Someone as low born as myself could never hope to be King Nøkkyn's wife. No, I was to be the newest addition to the Mountain King's harem, his fresh concubine.

His whore.

Ma had tried to prepare me.

"Don't ever disagree with him," she said, late one night, as we lay under our furs before the low flickering embers of the fire. "Try to make him laugh, but never at himself. Don't ever tell him no. About anything. And always smile, but try to save a special smile just for him."

I'd rolled my eyes, hoping the growing darkness in our house would hide my expression. King Nøkkyn did not seem the sort to be overly impressed by a special smile.

"And Sol, when he comes to you at night—"

I groaned as I turned away from her in the sleeping furs, trying to avoid any reason for my thoughts to swirl back to Nøkkyn's pinched, cruel face.

I'd heard about sex, of course. I'd seen it among the chickens and pigs. I'd shared sweet kisses with boys in the village, although they were all too high-born to consider me worthy of courting. I'd even felt the hard length of Bryn's manhood press against my stomach as his hips twitched while we danced beneath the colored lights at last year's Harvest Festival. That kiss had left me gasping, dreaming about my own marriage bed and wondering whose handsome face I'd find on the pillow next to mine in the morning. Or who I would see grunting and moaning above me at night.

King Nøkkyn's dark eyes and thin lips were not at all what I'd envisioned.

"Just..." Ma said, hesitantly. "Be sure he thinks you enjoy it. All of it. Whatever it is."

My stomach clenched at the thought of what Nøkkyn might want to do to me. "Was that how you had to treat Da?"

She fell silent, and I wished I could take back my harsh words. When Ma finally spoke again, her voice was low and sad.

"I don't have your beauty, Sol."

"Some prize beauty is," I muttered, "if I'm to be sold as a whore."

Her cold fingers wrapped around mine, squeezing my hand. "My daughter. You're saving us. You're buying us food and freedom. Please don't forget that."

I snorted. Some gift, trading in my freedom so my family could eke out another year in the cold shadow of the Ironwood forest.

"And you'll get to live in the palace," Ma had said, her voice a shade too high to be sincere. "You'll never go hungry, my dear."

I bit my lip and kicked a stone out of the path. My stomach churned along with my memories. Damn my stupid face. Damn my beauty. If I'd been born a man, I'd be in the woods now, felling purple oaks alongside my brothers instead of hauling the eggs to market. Blinking, I wiped away the stray tears. The rank unfairness of it burned me, the injustice that I had to get dressed up and painted and hauled away. If only Da hadn't died...

Da's voice echoed in my head. Don't chase the would-have-beens. And Ma was right. I might be going as a whore to King Nøkkyn's castle, but I wouldn't go hungry.

CHAPTER TWO

The beaten grass of the rutted road turned slowly to dirt, then to mud, as I approached town. The foul-smelling black earth squelched between my toes; my lip curled in distaste. Damn, what I wouldn't give for a pair of shoes. Suddenly, Maddie Liefsen's words echoed in my head. I'd overheard her talking with the other town girls during the last Harvest Festival. It was late at night, and multi colored lanterns burned in the branches above us. I'd spent the entire night trading dances with Bryn and the other handsome town boys, laughing as they spun me so quickly the flickering lanterns became a brilliant shimmering blur. Bryn had pulled me close and pressed his hips against mine until I felt the urgent heat of his manhood through the thin fabric of my dress. My own core thrummed in response, and I wished the music would never stop.

But the song ended, as everything must. I'd walked to the row of chairs in the grass to rest my feet while Bryn bought himself a horn of beer. Maddie was huddled with the other town girls, frowning at everything.

"Oh, yes, Sol dances with everyone," Maddie snapped, "but she's barefoot. Like a slave!"

Harsh laughter followed this observation. Some of my elation had leaked into the cold night air as I stared at my bare feet, dusty and sweat-stained from dancing. I wasn't entirely certain if Maddie had meant for me to overhear her. I wasn't sure what was worse, being the intentional target of her casual cruelty or being a barefoot eavesdropper. When Bryn returned, his eyes glazed with expensive beers from the drinking tent, I pled fatigue and turned him down. As I left the festival, I saw him dancing with Maddie, spinning her to the music, her silken shoes flashing in the lantern-light.

That was the way of it. I was far too low-born to be courted by a boy as rich as Bryn. He'd marry Maddie Liefsen, or one of her sniggering friends, and they'd dance together in the town square with shoes on their feet. It was no use wanting the world to be otherwise. Gather wishes in one hand and shit in the other, as my Da used to say. See which one fills up first.

I forced myself to stand tall when I saw the dull gray posts of Attin's fence, the first sign of human habitation since I'd left our farthest potato fields. The ramshackle collection of his farm buildings would follow, and then the first of the town buildings. I'd have to pass three of the fancy townhouses before reaching Johmaersen's bakery and, I hoped, the best price for Ma's eggs. Johmaersen had always been kind to me. At least before.

"Sol!"

I jumped at the voice. It sounded like a young man, and his intonation tugged at my memory. Was it one of the town boys, someone I'd recognize?

I turned and saw a tall figure step out from the shadows of Attin's barn. Bryn, I realized. It was Bryn Attinsen. The sun lingered low on the horizon during harvest season, casting sharp shadows across the landscape and making it hard to decipher the expression on his face. He took a step closer, and I told myself to relax. This was Bryn, for the star's sake. The boy who danced with me, who'd held me under the colored lights and kissed me until my head spun.

"Hello, Bryn!" I called. "You startled me!"

He smiled at my voice. In the days after last year's Harvest Festival, I'd allowed myself an occasional, impossible dream about what it would be like to have Bryn as my husband, to wake and find his handsome face on the other side of the pillow every morning.

Bryn stepped into the middle of the muddy road, his feet wide and one arm cocked behind his back. Only then did I notice something oddly cold about his smile. Shivers crept up my spine. A flash of motion caught my eye, and I spun to see another figure emerging from behind Attin's barn. He was a full head taller than Bryn, and he wore the same hard, cold smile. Both his arms were tucked behind his back.

I recognized him. Olafur. Once, when little Egren was only five or six, Olafur had chased him through town, pelting him with rocks until he bled. Da pulled us all aside and told us to run like deer if we ever saw Olafur again.

"You'll be safe under the trees," Da had told us, his voice rough and his eyes dark. "You kids belong to the Ironwood. They'll never find you in here."

I shifted uncertainly on my feet, not daring to glance behind me. I wasn't far from the shelter of the Ironwood, but the basket of eggs pressed against my hip, heavy and unforgiving. Ma was right; we needed the flour. I forced myself to stand tall and ignore the tight knot in my gut.

"Hello, Olafur," I said, willing my voice not to tremble.

"Sol." His voice was a lazy, slow drawl. "What a surprise."

"We hear you've been sold," said Bryn.

His voice was different. It had been honey and velvet when we kissed during the Harvest festival. Now it was steel.

"Bryn?" My voice trembled as I spoke, and I wished I could bite back the word.

"Sol." He gave me a smile that made me feel all the warmth had been drained from the world.

I glanced at Olafur's cruel, pale eyes and then back to Bryn, trying to force my lips to smile. "I thought we were—"

The words died in my throat. I thought we were what? Friends? Bryn and I had never played at being friends.

"Oh, you thought we were?" Bryn said, throwing my words back at me as if they'd been a sardonic joke.

Bryn stepped closer, one hand still held behind his back, and dropped his eyes to crawl over the swell of my breasts. "Pretty little Sol from the mud of the backwoods. Sol, who'll let any boy put their hand up her skirts."

Mud squelched between my toes as I shifted my weight, pulling the eggs even closer to my body.

"We had a bet going, you know. Between the boys. To see who'd be the first to break your pretty little maidenhead wide open."

His grin vanished, and his eyes hardened. "Now, you've gone and sold it to the highest bidder."

"I didn't have much of a say—" I stammered.

Olafur snorted, loudly, and I fell silent. He spat a great wad of phlegm into the mud of the road. "We don't like whores in town, Sol."

"I-I've brought eggs to sell. For Johmaersen."

Something moved along Attin's fence post, and I glanced to the side. Two more boys were pulling themselves through the gray slats of the fence. They looked like the Bergensen twins, but I couldn't be certain. I'd never seen the Bergensen twins wear such predatory smiles, or look at me with such hard, cold eyes. The first tendrils of real panic began to tighten around my chest.

"Bryn," I pleaded, meeting his eyes. "I'm just taking eggs to—"

Something wet and cold slapped my face. I staggered backward, wiping my eyes. My hands came away black with mud. Olafur guffawed as a streak of mud trailed down the pale blue front of my everyday dress.

"What—" I stammered.

Bryn pulled back his arm and something dark flew through the air. It hit me in the open mouth. The cold grit of mud coated my tongue, and I gagged, staggering backward.

The basket of eggs hit something behind me with a sickening crunch. I flinched and turned. Yes, it was indeed the Bergensen twins. Now they stood like great pillars behind me. I used to think they looked kind, with their pale eyes and straw-colored hair, but there was no kindness in their expression today.

"Whore," one of them said, pushing me forward.

I staggered, almost hitting Bryn. Blinking through the mud that lay splattered across my face, I tried to speak. Something hard hit the back of my skull. My head exploded in a shock of blinding, white pain.

"You don't look so pretty now, little whore," Bryn sneered.

His big hands shoved my shoulders. I slipped in the mud and crashed to the ground. My hands and tailbone shrieked with pain. My fingers scrambled over the woven straps of the basket, and I tried to pull the eggs onto my lap where I could curl my body around them.

Someone kicked me in the ribs, sending bright bolts of pain up my abdomen. I doubled over in the filth of the road, the eggs forgotten.

"Dirty whore," Olafur snorted.

Fistfulls of mud and stones rained down on me. Over the ringing in my ears, I heard the merry echos of their laugher.

"She looks like a pig in shit," one of the Bergensen twins announced.

"She smells like a pig in shit!" Olafur snorted, apparently laughing at his own joke.

"Some whore," Bryn announced. "She's not worth a copper."

Someone's foot slammed down on my shin. I ground my teeth together, not wanting to give them the satisfaction of a scream.

"She's not worth a piss," Olafur laughed.

Oh, by the Realms.

"No," I cried. "Please, no!"

Something hot splashed against my chest, and I couldn't stop my scream. I recoiled, twisting to get away, and rolled onto my side. Someone's sharp, hard shoe connected with the small of my back, and I heard the sharp crack of the egg basket as it flattened beneath my hips. Something thick and wet rolled down my shoulder, but whether it was eggs or piss was impossible to tell. A second stream hit my ribs, the hot liquid trickling through my thin dress and between my breasts, and a third landed on the curve of my stomach. I covered my face and tried to breathe through the mud while I waited for them to finish, willing myself not to cry.

Not here. Not in front of them.

Finally, Bryn stopped laughing long enough to speak. "Don't come back," he cried. "Whores aren't welcome here."

The men laughed again, even louder this time, and I heard the flat ring of shoulders being slapped in celebration. Then the dull thud of shoes as they turned to walk away, laughing. I caught snatches of their conversation.

"Nice aim, Bryn. You–"

"Dumb whore. Good thing you saw her coming—"

"—a pint together?"

When their voices finally faded and I could hear the call and murmur of the birds again, I lifted my head and took my first shuddering breath. Then I forced myself to count to one hundred before I opened my eyes.

There was nothing before me but the flat muck of the road. I wiped dirt from my eyes and pulled the basket from the reeking, gritty mess beneath me. It was shattered. I pawed through the mud and piss and broken twigs, searching for a single intact egg.

There were none.

Every egg had been broken. The dark mass of snapped twigs that had once been Ma's woven basket gleamed with slick albumen and tiny, delicate fragments of eggshell. A dark and furious rage boiled inside me as I thought of my mother dragging her busted leg to the hen house. Collecting those eggs.

Something flickered in the corner of my eye, and I turned. Someone vanished behind Attin's barn. Someone tall.

Tall as Attin himself.

My rage fled before an even stronger force. Shame. Had Attin watched what Bryn and those boys had done to me, or was he just now coming around the corner of his barn? My heart hammered against my chest, and my skin felt hot. Having Attin see me like this, covered in mud and piss and shattered eggs, would make my humiliation unbearable. Bryn may have thought me a filthy whore, but stars, that didn't mean the rest of the village had to see me like this.

I forced myself to my feet, clutching the shattered bits of the basket in my hands. My ankle screamed at first, but the pain dulled as I took a few steps. Thank the Realms. If those town boys had broken my ankle, I'd really be trapped. After a few steps, the pain in my side ebbed and I found I could run.

I could even run while I cried.

CHAPTER THREE

The Körmt River has many tributaries. One of them, the Jorgyn, runs through the village, and the Jorgyn in turn is nurtured by a stream that flows past our home and down by our potato fields. It's such a tiny little thing, I've never known if it even has a name. My Da always called it the Lucky; I was never sure if he meant it as a joke.

I ran through the Ironwood until I found the soft, winding banks of the Lucky, and there I stumbled and fell to my knees, panting hard. The Lucky ran slow and dark on the edges of the Ironwood, winding through a series of pebble-lined pools. Insects buzzed over its dark waters, and birds called to one another through the canopy. I held still for a long time, listening for the sound of pursuers.

Once I was sure I was alone, I slipped out of my dress and into the dark waters of that slow little river. The biting cold of the water was a relief after running for so long. I picked up handfuls of gravel from the riverbed and ran it over my arms and legs until my skin was red and raw, wishing I could scrub away my memories so easily.

Only when my hands and feet began to ache from cold did I step out of the water and turn to my dress. Like the basket, my dress was ruined. It would forever be stained, and it may never again smell of anything other than piss and mud.

Still, I had to try.

I sank the threadbare fabric deep in the tannin-rich waters, and I was sorely tempted to let it swirl away on the slow currents. But it was bad enough I'd be returning home with no flour, no eggs, and no basket. I didn't want to come home naked, too.

I dragged my dress over the stones of the river bottom and ground pebbles into the fabric, imagining I was grinding those sharp stones into the faces of those village boys. Only when my hands were numb from the cold did I pull the dripping fabric from the dark river. It was late in the afternoon, and the light filtering through the forest canopy was thick and golden. Little white flies rose from the swirling waters, stretching their wings before fluttering upward.

I brought the fabric to my nose and took a deep breath. It smelled of darkness and pine tannins, with the metallic tang of cold, fresh water. Not eggs, or piss.

Or humiliation.

The fabric was still streaked with dark stains from the mud, but at least the smell was gone. I could live with that. With a sigh, I lay my dress on the grass beside the water. It wasn't going to dry this late in the day; no matter what, my walk home would be cold and uncomfortable. But I could at least give myself some time here, in the protection of the woods, before I had to explain what happened to the eggs.

I closed my eyes, tilted my face toward the fading sunlight, and ran my fingers through my wet hair, carefully avoiding the sore lump on the back of my skull. The fear and shame of the day slowly melted from my body, evaporating in the thick evening light. I was safe under the trees, just like Da always said.

I can scarcely explain what made me turn.

There were no strange noises, nothing out of the ordinary. The river hissed and murmured. Birds cried from the canopy while the wind whispered to the treetops. Shadows pooled beneath the pines' thick trunks, and the evening insects began their songs.

Still, something silent and invisible thickened the air, raising the hairs on the back of my neck. I opened my eyes and turned away from the Lucky, toward the deep forest.

He stood a pace away from me, beneath the trees. Not hiding, but not exactly visible. He was so motionless, he may as well have been made of wood himself. My heart jumped, and I grabbed a river-smooth stone in my fist before coming to my feet. If he tried to throw mud at me, I'd smash that stone into his skull.

His pale eyes blinked, and he tilted his head to the side as if trying to understand what he was seeing. My breath caught in my throat. He wore no shirt; black curls of hair scattered across the rippling muscles of his chest. His bare skin reminded me of my own nakedness, and my cheeks warmed.

"Who are you?" I demanded.

He frowned, then tilted his head to the other side.

"Are you from the village?" I asked. My voice trembled slightly as I tightened my fingers around the cool rock pressed to my palm. I'd never seen him before, but that meant little. Town people moved around like seeds on the wind.

"No." His voice sounded odd, as though he were unused to speaking. "I am not from the village."

My fingers relaxed around the smooth stone from the riverbank. He wasn't one of the boys from the village, come to further torment me. Thank the stars. I glanced down at my stained, wet dress spread over the grass, then at my own exposed body. I'd never been naked in front of a stranger before. King Nøkkyn most certainly would not approve. The thought sent an unexpected ripple of heat through my core.

"I'm not decent," I said, wrapping an arm around my breasts and cupping my free hand over the curls between my legs.

His gaze dropped, as though he were just now noticing I was completely naked. He watched me for a long time, his eyes widening as they traveled down my arms, over my legs, and along the bare contours of my hips. My skin warmed as he watched me, almost as though he were running his elegant fingers across my body, chasing away the cold of the Lucky's waters.

"You're quite beautiful," he said at last when his light eyes returned to my face.

Beautiful. How many times had I heard that? Ever since I was a child, I'd been dogged by that word. I'd grown to hate it.

But, coming from his soft, full lips, the word brought me pleasure. Beautiful. It was unreasonable, but I was glad to hear he found me beautiful. My lips started to curve, and I turned away, embarrassed to have the stranger see me smile.

"Excuse me," I said.

I bent toward the grass and let the rock slip from my fingers when I grabbed my dress. It was still wet, but I pushed it to my chest anyway, making sure the damp, stained cloth covered my breasts before I stood again.

He'd moved. The stranger was one step closer to me. I blinked, trying not to stare at the way his muscles curved and arched toward his hips. He was totally naked, and I had to force myself to tear my eyes away before they could linger between his legs.

Was he mad? Was this a demon from the fiery depths of Múspell?

He was certainly handsome enough to be a demon, with his pale eyes and high cheekbones. His hair spread over his shoulders, a dark amber like the last flash of life in a dying fire. A tiny green twig twisted in the strands. Something unexpected tightened deep inside me as the silence between us stretched taut.

Perhaps he was trying to lure me toward him, so he could grab me around the waist and drag me back to Múspell. I watched him through narrowed eyes, wondering about Múspell. How would his demon fires compare to the cold stone of King Nøkkyn's fortress?

I'd never seen the fortress of Nøkkyn the Mountain King, of course, but everything I'd ever heard about it was frightening. Some of it was downright terrifying, like the stories of rotting heads on iron spikes lining the gates. Even the head of his first wife, if the rumors were true. Could life with the demons of Múspell possibly be any worse?

If this strange madman dragged me away, I'd look at those bright blue eyes every day, those full lips and high cheekbones, that thick, auburn hair swirling around his temples. My heart thrummed against my breastbone so loudly I worried he'd hear it.

"What do you want?" My voice wavered like sunlight across the water.

"Want?" he echoed. He frowned, and a crease appeared between his ice-blue eyes. It made him look older.

"Are you a demon?" I asked.

His frown deepened until he looked slightly lost. "Why would I be a demon?"

I shook my head, pressing my lips together to keep from answering his question. Because you're so beautiful, I wanted to say. Because you're naked, in the middle of the Ironwood, by yourself.

"I-I'm sorry. Have I scared you?" he asked.

"No," I said, crushing my dress to my chest as if it could muffle the wild pounding of my heart.

"Don't run. Please."

"I won't," I promised.

I didn't want to run. I didn't want to put any more space between the two of us, between his bare chest and arms and my trembling body.

He closed his eyes and took a deep breath, his nostrils flaring. His lips twitched as he opened his eyes, almost as though he were trying to remember how to smile.

"I'm Fenris," he said.

I couldn't stop my laugh. It rang across the Lucky like a peal of thunder before I could clamp my hand over my lips. He frowned again, his forehead wrinkling.

"I'm sorry," I said. "But Fenris is a wolf. A monster. You're just a boy."

"A boy?"

He took another step toward me, so close I could have touched him, then glanced down at himself. A flash of heat burned through my body. No, not a boy. His shoulders were wide, and his chest was ridged with muscles. And between his legs...This close, I couldn't avoid it. I didn't want to avoid it. Another ripple of heat surged deep inside me as I drank in the sight of him.

I'd seen my brothers and father naked, on occasion, the drooping, pale stem between their legs curled around the wrinkled sack holding their seed. Those markers of their manhood had seemed oddly soft and vulnerable, almost comic.

But this demon was different. There was nothing vulnerable about what stood between his legs, hard, straight, and alarmingly large, jutting from a tangle of thick curls to point directly at the evening sky. I was suddenly very aware of my wet dress pressed against my breasts and between my legs, its thin fabric and the thick air the only things separating our two bodies.

I dragged my eyes back to his face. His soft lips curved over white teeth as I met his eyes. He had a strangely pleasant smile. I wondered if his lips would feel as soft as they looked, and blood rushed to my cheeks as the space between my legs grew even warmer.

"But, you're not a monster," I insisted. "You have a stick in your hair."

He frowned and ran his fingers through his hair, just missing the little twig as it twisted above his ear.

"No, your other side," I said.

I pinned my dress under an arm, reached for him, and pulled the tiny branch from his long, auburn curls. He caught my wrist. My heart surged, hammering against my ribcage. He turned, his lips almost brushing my skin. His nostrils flared and his eyes closed. I forgot to breathe.

"Your scent," he growled. "I know you. You like to pick the bloodberries along the river."

"Y-yes," I stammered.

My skin burned under his cool touch. I did like bloodberries, the little red spheres that grew only along shady riverbanks. And yes, I'd picked baskets full in the early summer. I picked the last harvest just a month ago, not far from here.

His lips pressed against the inside of my wrist. They felt as soft as I'd imagined. I shivered, although I was far from cold. A strange heat filled me, a burning born of some new fire I'd never before touched. I opened my mouth to say something, to ask who he was and what he was doing with his lips to make my body smolder like this but, instead of speaking, I moaned like an animal.

His gaze met mine, and he smiled.

I wasn't sure who moved first, if he came toward me or if I was drawn to him like a moth to a candle, but when he released my wrist I was in his arms with my wet dress pressed between my breasts and the hard muscles of his bare chest. I was half surprised the heat of our bodies didn't release a cloud of steam from the fabric.

I tilted my head. I wanted him to kiss me. I needed that kiss, needed it the way the trees need sunlight and rainwater.

He wrapped his arms around my waist, and I felt the hard jut of his manhood against my stomach. I'd never been told the exact mechanics of what it was men and women did together in the darkness of their sleeping furs, but on some level my body understood what it wanted. My thighs slicked with heat and moisture; my hips tilted toward him, seeking him, needing him.

He buried his face in my hair, his breath hot against my neck as he ran his hands over my waist and up my back.

"Smells good," he muttered. "Oh, you smell good."

He pulled back, then dropped to his knees. I gasped, missing the heat of his chest against mine. The sudden absence felt like pain.

I looked down at his pale eyes. He raised a trembling hand to my chest, and his fingers curled around my wet, crushed dress.

"Yes," I whispered.

He peeled it from my chest and stomach and tossed it to the ground. The demon stared at me as if he'd never seen a woman before, as if he could devour me with his eyes. Shivers chased flashes of heat across my skin, and my body cried out for him, although I could not have voiced exactly what it was I wanted. Energy surged from my core, and the space between my legs ached in a way it had never ached before.

He brushed his fingers along the backs of my thighs, and I moaned. He leaned even closer, breathing deeply, bringing his face to the curls between my legs.

"Your scent," he said in a voice that was almost a sigh. "I've smelled you in the forest, and I've searched and searched for you."

When his lips brushed the skin my thigh, the sensation was so intense it almost hurt. I panted, whimpering like a trapped animal. His tongue touched me, tracing the wet split of my sex, and my vision drowned in a red haze. I fell against his strong arms, his thick chest. He lowered me to the grass as my mind whirled and spun, trying to make sense of what was happening.

He crouched above me, grinning. Slowly, the demon bent to kiss the soft skin on the inside of my thigh. His head vanished between my legs; he moaned into my sex as his tongue slipped inside me.

Oh, by the Nine Realms. He was eating me. The demon was eating me alive.

I'd never heard of such a thing, never known it was possible. It seemed wrong somehow, wild and bizarre, like a secret the demon brought with him from Múspell. My hips rippled under his strange kiss, moving of their own volition. He had taken over my body, making it blaze and dance; he'd erased my control.

"Don't," I gasped. "Don't stop."

I reached for his head, lacing my fingers in his thick hair. It felt so damned good, this demon's kiss between my legs. Stars, nothing had ever felt so good—

His tongue found something different, something I hadn't even known existed, and pleasure as intense as lightning seared me from the inside. I screamed as my body exploded beneath him, my back arching to jam my hips against his lips, my hands writhing in his thick hair. He pulled back, and I closed my legs, forcing him against me.

The demon's tongue pressed the spot again, and again. The world dissolved in heat and ecstasy. My last coherent thought was that I must be dying, the demon had somehow killed me with his lips between my legs, and then every thought I'd ever had was washed away.

CHAPTER FOUR

High above me, the rich green treetops undulated slowly in the thick evening light. I blinked. Perhaps, I wasn't dead after all. But oh, I felt so strange! Like I'd been burned away and then rebuilt. I was just now surfacing, floating on still waters. Fingers brushed my cheek. I turned to follow them. The demon's pale eyes watched me below a furrowed brow.

"I'm sorry," he said. "Did I hurt you?"

For the second time, I couldn't stop my laugh. It rang through the gloaming like bells, dancing across the Lucky River and entering the darkness of the Iron-wood.

"Oh, by the Realms!" I gasped. "No. No, you didn't hurt me."

"I've never heard anyone make noises like that."

I laughed again. "Well, it didn't hurt."

His soft lips turned downward, deepening his frown, and once again I couldn't resist him. I grabbed his neck and pulled his lips to mine. He froze, then softened as we came together. The demon kissed me slowly, as though he were exploring an unfamiliar room for the first time, in the dark. His kisses were salty and rich, like sweat and earth.

We lay together for a long time, our tongues embracing. He was beside me at first, then he moved on top of me. The thick length of his manhood pulsed between my slick thighs. The slow heat he inspired filled my body again, beginning between my legs and growing to engulf all of me, flowing from his lips and tongue and fingers. Our hips began to move, surging together, and I felt the blunt, hot tip of his manhood against the wet heat of my sex. I moaned something incoherent, voicing a hunger beyond words, and opened my legs beneath him.

His arms stiffened, and he broke our kiss. Slowly, he raised his body above mine. The air that rushed between us felt icy after the heat of our embrace.

"Do you want more?" he asked.

I pulled breath over my lips. Time seemed to have frozen, and suddenly I was strangely aware of everything around me; the slow tickle of grass behind my ear, the ripple of wind bending the high, bright branches above us, the susurrus of his breath above me. My body glowed with pleasure from our kisses, and the aching fire he'd just ignited still roared inside me. I wanted him to touch me, to run his hands over my breasts, to plunge them between my legs.

No, not just his hands. The hard length of his cock pressed between my legs as if it were trying to force its own way forward. And the space between my thighs throbbed in response, aching and empty. I wanted him, damn the Realms. I wanted that heat, that power, that strength. I wanted to feel him inside me, to finally know what it was the high-born town girls whispered and giggled about at dances.

Yes. I wanted more.

I opened my mouth, but a cold uncertainty rose in the back of my throat and choked my words. My body wasn't mine to give. Nøkkyn's sharp features rose in my memories, dousing the fire this demon's touch had just kindled inside me.

I was goods. Property.

The demon watched me, his brow furrowed. His body no longer moved against mine; now he'd frozen above me, our legs intertwined, the air between us still hot with our frantic, panting breath. Above him, leaves swirled in the fading light.

I turned away from his sharp, pale eyes. Dark tree trunks lined the banks of the Lucky River, crowding out the light. For a moment, they made me think of a cage. Something hard and painful rose inside my chest.

Da once told me kings and queens of old captured birds from the Ironwood and forced them into golden cages to make the echoing halls of their palaces echo with the songs of the wilderness. I'd cried when I thought of those birds, so far from home, surrounded by cold, gleaming bars instead of living tree boughs, and Da laughed at my foolish tears. He told me the imprisoned birds had food and warmth, that they had traded their songs for shelter. Still, for years, the thought of birds in elegant, gilded cages made my chest tighten.

I remembered Nøkkyn's cruel smile, the sour tang of his sweat in my nostrils as he pulled my hair back, and a dark fury rose inside me.

I wasn't his yet.

I didn't want King Nøkkyn, or his thrice-damned fortress. Curse his golden cage, his food and warmth! I wanted this demon to touch me again, to make my body sing and cry. I wanted to give myself over, here, now, to burn what was left of my freedom in the fires of his touch.

Let me choose my own lover! Let me sing my song of pleasure beneath the trees of the Ironwood while I still could! If going to Múspell as a demon's consort was the price of that choice, well, the fiery realms could not possibly be worse than King Nøkkyn's harem. The fiery realms would contain those pale eyes, those soft lips and gentle kisses, the pulsing heat of his sex above mine.

"Yes," I whispered.

His eyes widened as I spread my thighs and wrapped my legs around his waist.

"Take me," I said. My breath caught in my throat before I could add *to Múspell.*

Sinking my fingers into his hair, I pulled his lips back to mine. He kissed me again, long and slow and deep, until we were trading breaths. Then he shifted above me; the hard head of his cock pulsed between my legs. His breath hitched, and he hesitated.

"Yes!" I cried.

He bit his lip and pressed closer. I arched my back to meet him, giving him what King Nøkkyn had claimed, giving it to him without a moment's hesitation.

There was pain, of course. Ma had warned me there would be pain, and blood, when I surrendered my maidenhead. But after the pain was a sense of being filled, of being whole. And beyond that was a blinding rush of pleasure so intense I cried out, telling him yes, more, give me more!

He moved inside me slowly and carefully. Stars, he felt so good! I laughed and cried at the same time, crossing my ankles over his back as though I'd fall apart without him. He groaned as he lowered his face to my neck, where his breath sent shivers skating across my bare skin.

Our hips began to move together without thought or volition, carried away by the tides our bodies created. His back slicked with sweat, and his breath turned into gasping cries. He sank his fingers into my hair, curving his body above mine as his thrusts grew deeper and less rhythmic. When his back stiffened above me and he cried like an animal, I realized I'd given him the same obliterating ecstasy he had shown me.

I laughed.

In his arms, as the light faded beneath the waving limbs of the trees, I laughed until tears ran down my cheeks. When I finally caught my breath and turned to smile at him, I found he was watching me closely with a frown etched across his handsome features.

"You laugh quite often," he said.

I grinned at his somber tone. "And you frown a lot."

His frown deepened. "I do not."

"You're frowning right now!"

He moved the hand that had been cupping my breast and ran it across his face. Then he turned back to me with the hint of a smile playing across his lips.

"I'm sorry," he said. "I'm not unhappy."

His lips curved hesitantly, as if they were trying to remember how to smile. By the Realms, he was handsome. He had to be a demon; none of the boys in the village looked this good when they smiled. I sighed and shifted on the grass, pressing my body closer to his.

"So, are you of Múspell?" I asked. If only I could remember the stories. Did I have to ask three times or guess his name to bind him?

He laughed. His voice was low and thick, as though he were unused to laughing. "Demons again? Why would you say that?"

"You're so beautiful." The words slipped from my lips before I could stop them.

He turned away, but not before I saw his smile widen.

"Can you at least tell me your name?" I pleaded.

He shifted on the grass, turning to rest on his elbows. I missed the warmth of his body against mine; already the night air felt colder.

"I did tell you my name."

"Oh. Right." I smiled at the absurdity of his claim. "Well, if you're the Fenris-wolf, then I'm Queen Hel, mighty and terrible ruler of Niflhel."

He laughed again, a little easier this time. "You look nothing like my sister."

Of course. I'd forgotten Queen Hel and the Fenris-wolf were siblings, both the children of Loki the Lie-smith and Angrboða, Duchess of the Black Isle, She-who-brings-sorrow.

"Well, if you are the monster wolf of the Ironwood, I suppose you can run down King Nøkkyn and rip his head off?"

There was still enough light for me to see him arch his eyebrow. "So you're beautiful and bloodthirsty? What is King Nøkkyn to you that you want him dead?"

I opened my mouth. Suddenly, I remembered the sting of mud in my eyes and the grit of it spread over my tongue. The way Bryn's eyes glinted in the sun just before he called me *whore*.

And now I'd just spread my legs for a stranger in the woods.

Perhaps I really was a whore.

"Nothing," I muttered. I rolled away from him and pushed myself to my feet.

"Do you have a place where you need to be?" he asked.

His eyes burned in the gloaming. My mind spun; my skin was too hot and too cold all at the same time. Did this mean he wasn't going to drag me to Múspell and claim me for his own? I tore my eyes away from his, half afraid of what I'd say if I kept staring at his beautiful face.

"I need to get home," I said. My lips felt numb.

My dress was wet and cold when I plucked it off the grass, but my mind burned, and I was almost thankful for the press of the cool fabric against my skin. I pulled it over my head, wincing slightly at a new ache deep inside my abdomen. The enormity of what I'd just done loomed before me, as vast and cold and unforgiving as the Körmt river.

The demon watched me, his face upturned. "I can walk with you."

The swirling darkness inside me abated somewhat as I met his gaze. How could he do that, I marveled. How could he bring me peace with just a glance? Had I truly been bewitched?

I shook my head. "I'm fine."

"It's night." His frown returned, chasing away his earlier, tentative smile. "Aren't you afraid to walk alone?"

A delicate shiver danced along my spine. "No."

He stood and ran his fingers over the back of his neck. "I see. Well, would you perhaps be more unafraid if I were to join you?"

I tried not to smile and failed. "Perhaps."

"Then I'll join you." His teeth flashed in the fading light as he grinned at me.

I glanced at the pale muscles of his naked body. "Don't you want to get dressed first?"

"Dressed? Whatever for?"

He took my arm, and I laughed again. He had to be a demon, or a madman. Possibly both. But when he pulled me to his side and smiled, his clothing and his name, what we'd just done and what may come of it, all ceased to matter.

CHAPTER FIVE

"Are there people in Ironwood?" I asked Ma as casually as I could manage. She'd been unusually gentle with me in the five days since I had stumbled home in the dark, without flour or eggs, my dress still wet from the Lucky and my head reeling from the demon's kisses. She fed me turnip and potato soup, with thick slices of the bread she'd made with the last of our flour, and she didn't even ask me what had happened in town.

Ma's eyes went a bit misty over the yarn she was spooling. "There used to be more people. Before Lvardsen went to war in Agoria, and Etna passed on."

I shook my head. "No, not people like us. I mean, are there people living in the Ironwood?"

The corners of her mouth crinkled. "Worried about your brothers, are you?"

A hot flush of shame raced through my body. Yes, I should be worried about my brothers. I should not be thinking constantly about what's between my legs, and how a demon in the forest made me feel like I was going to die of pleasure.

"There's no one who lives in the Ironwood," Ma said, "and I would know. I used to go with your father, remember? We'd go for weeks in the Ironwood, and we never found another soul." She bent to bite off a thread. "So, no fears. There's no one to harm your brothers."

I shook my head, trying to bring my focus back to the pile of clothing in my lap. Today, Ma was spooling yarn for hats, and I was mending tattered rags, trying to make jackets for my brothers in the bright sun of late summer. But my mind had wandered, and my stitches went wild. If she noticed, Ma said nothing.

I'd thought of nothing but him for the past five days.

The chatter of the Lucky past our far potato fields reminded me of his laugh. The thin streak of pale sky at daybreak was the same shade as his eyes.

Once, when Ma and I were harvesting button mushrooms along the dark fringe of Ironwood, I swore I could even smell him. I'd been bent toward the earth, my fingers brushing aside the loose pine duff of the forest floor, when the hairs along my neck prickled almost as though a hand had caressed my skin. But when I turned to stare at the darkness beneath the pines, I'd seen nothing but the play of light and shadows across the smattering of ferns behind me. I almost called his name, but Ma cried for me, and I'd come back to reality.

And, oh, how my body ached for his touch! In the dark, silent hours of the night, I waited until I was certain Ma was asleep, and then I brought my hands between my legs, trying to touch myself the way he had touched me. The pleasure I stole during those furtive, panting moments was sharp and intense, but still just a distant echo of the ecstasy his body gave me. Almost always, after the crest of pleasure, tears slid past my closed eyelids in the dark, chasing my bliss.

"You're sure?" I pushed. "What about...demons?"

Ma finally sighed and put down her yarn. "Sol, demons are a child's fear. This is the real world, not some story from Bard Sturlinsen. You know demons do not leave Múspell."

I turned to the ground, feeling my cheeks burn. As though she'd be able to sense my guilt just by meeting my eyes.

"If you'd like to speak about what happened in town—" Ma began.

"No." I stood, folding the rags in my chair to cover my trembling hands. "I'll go tend to the potatoes."

She sighed again. "Take your time. I know you've little enough time left here."

Her words did not bring me comfort.

THE HEAVY SUMMER SUN was falling toward the trees when I reached our potato field. It was the furthest field from our house, and the closest to the banks of the Lucky, where the soil was richest. It did not need weeding; this late in the year, the potato plants were tall and strong, far more massive than any of the weeds.

But I'd brought the hoe anyway, and I plunged it into the rich, dark earth, severing the roots of bindweed and the bitter tanglewood shoots. I wanted to be alone, working hard with my entire body, leaving no room for my mind to spin.

He had to have been a demon of Múspell, but my traitorous brain wouldn't accept reality. I kept dreaming he was a prince or a prisoner; a madman or a mystic. Perhaps I could rescue him from a spell, like in one of the stories they say Bard Sturlinsen sang when the world was young.

Perhaps he could rescue me.

I wiped sweat from my eyes and attacked a huge patch of bindweed. It was far enough from the potatoes that it wasn't a threat to their fecundity, but it was satisfying to hack the little green stems into nothingness. The air filled with the tang of their crushed leaves. Useless damned weeds.

Little enough time, Ma said. She was right. King Nøkkyn would claim me on the day of the Harvest Festival, taking me to the black towers of his fortress, a place none of us had ever seen. And then he'd find the woman he claimed and bought was—

"Hello."

I jumped. The hoe's thick handle flew from my fingers to crash against the earth. My heart raced, and I gulped for air as I turned toward the shadows of the Ironwood.

He stood on the edge of the potato field, his dark red hair swirling around his shoulders, his pale eyes burning. My vision blurred with wholly unexplainable tears as he walked toward me. His bare foot sank into the dark earth and broken bindweed stems.

"You," I gasped.

He nodded. He was so close I could have fallen into his arms and pressed my body against his naked chest.

"Everywhere I go, I smell you," he said. His voice was thick and rough. "Even in my dreams."

My breath caught in my throat. He raised his hand to gently brush my cheek.

"You've enchanted me," he said.

"No," I whispered. "No, I swear it."

He tilted his head to one side, running his eyes over my body. My skin prickled with heat; something deep and hungry inside me tightened.

"You're the one who's enchanted me," I said. "You're all I can think about."

He frowned. "I cast no spell."

"You wouldn't have to. You're a demon."

"You still think me a demon?"

His frown faded as he grinned, and my body grew noticeably warmer. Especially the place between my legs, the place I rubbed at night as I thought of him.

"You have to be." Now I felt my cheeks flushing as well. "No one else could be so handsome."

His smile widened. "You find me handsome?"

"Of course."

"You are the most beautiful woman in all the Realms," he said.

His voice was level, almost cold. He wasn't trying to impress me, I realized. He was stating a fact. The sun rises in the East. Winter's bitter cold follows summer's heat.

You are beautiful.

I met his eyes. He stared at me like the entire world contained only my body, my smile. He stared at me like he would die without me.

"I can't stop thinking of you," he said. "I—I want more."

He didn't even touch me. He didn't need to; his eyes set my body aflame. I opened my mouth and whispered the word my heart had sung since we met.

"Yes."

CHAPTER SIX

I had the presence of mind to insist we leave the field.

Even though everything else in the world had ceased to matter, even though I found it almost impossible to think with the fire of arousal consuming my body, some small, still reasonable part of my mind realized we should not fall upon each other in the middle of my family's potato field.

"How did you do it?" he asked as we walked toward the protection of the forest's thick shadows.

"Do what?"

"Cast your spell. You don't smell like magic."

I staggered as my feet found a grass-entrapped log. He caught me, pulling me to his chest.

"I-I didn't," It was a struggle to concentrate this close to his naked body. I could feel the hard length between his legs, and my body ached for it. "I'm not magical."

He took a deep breath and plunged his fingers into my hair. "I've never wanted more before."

My heart gave a strange little twinge at that, although I couldn't explain why.

"Once more," he whispered. "Just one more time."

My stomach fluttered. One more time suited me. My time in the shadow of the Ironwood was, after all, severely limited. Perhaps I could learn something from this demon, and show King Nøkkyn some new pleasure that would gain me favor.

"One more time," I agreed.

He sighed and his chest pressed against mine. His hands trembled as they ran down my back, fumbling with my dress. I helped him unlatch the clasp at the neck, careful to keep from tearing the threadbare fabric.

When the clasp opened, I stepped back and slipped the dress over my shoulders to pool at my feet. He moaned as if he'd been hurt.

"What's wrong?" I asked, glancing down to see if he'd stepped on something sharp.

I flushed again. His cock was enormous, and it had turned a rich shade of red, almost a violet. As I watched, a clear drop formed on the head, making something deep inside of me growl in hunger.

"Nothing," he groaned. "Everything."

He moved closer, running his hands over my arms. "Your scent. It's—Oh, stars, it's too much."

I opened my mouth to speak, but my body moved faster than my mind, and my lips pressed to his. I ran my fingers down the rippling muscles of his stomach, his dark hair rasping against my palm. When I reached his hips, I stopped thinking. I opened for him as our mouths embraced, letting his lips and tongue fill me while my fingers explored the differences in our bodies. He gasped into my mouth when I first brushed the hard length of his manhood, and I stopped, pulling back.

"Oh, no," he cried. "Stars, don't stop."

I smiled and stepped back into his arms, both my kisses and my touch more confident now. I ran my fingertips over the length of his cock, from its silky head to its thick base. His breath came faster, and his hips began to rock. I watched as his head tilted back.

Oh, he was handsome, this demon! My body burned next to his, and the space between my legs slicked with heat. The sheer power I held over him in this moment, the ability to make him tremble and pant and moan, flooded my mind.

He was so beautiful. So beautiful, and mine.

I wrapped my fingers around his length, gripping his shaft the same way my body had embraced him on the banks of the Lucky, and I moved my hand up and down, mimicking the cadence of his hips against mine.

"Yes," he said. "Yes, oh! Yes!"

His legs stiffened, pressing his weight against me, and I moved my hand faster, not entirely certain if that was what he wanted, or where this would lead. His arms tightened around my shoulders, and his entire body began to shake. His cock throbbed in my hands, and he cried out, his voice sounding off the trees. Heat exploded from the head of his cock and coated my belly. His shoulders sagged as he leaned against me.

"Sol," he whispered. "Oh, stars, Sol."

"You know my name." I flushed with pleasure at that small sign of intimacy.

He hummed something noncommittal as his lips found my neck, kissing the skin under my ear. The fire inside me flared at his touch.

"Tell me yours," I said.

"Fenris," he growled.

I opened my mouth to disagree, but he dropped to his knees in front of me, taking my nipple into his mouth, and all I could do was gasp. His lips and tongue were so delicate, flickering across the swell of my breast, kissing the hard bud of my nipple. He closed his eyes, breathing me in as he wrapped his hands around my thighs.

"I watched you," he said. "I followed your scent here. But you weren't alone."

My breath caught in my throat. So he had been there when Ma and I picked the button mushrooms.

"That's how you know my name," I whispered.

"Sol. Yes. It's a lovely name."

His head rested against my belly, next to the drying smear of seed he'd streaked over my abdomen, and his words sent shivers across my skin. I reached for his head, running my fingers through the wild tangles of his dark red hair. He smelled good, a thick, rich, male scent, like the forest personified.

"My demon," I whispered.

He grinned. His soft lips looked so inviting that I couldn't resist. I fell to my knees next to him, bringing my mouth to his. We kissed for a long time, our chests pressed together, our fingers intertwining. We kissed as his manhood grew hard again, first twitching tentatively against the smooth skin of my stomach, and then reaching urgently as his hips swayed into mine. We kissed until the world fell away, until the only thing that mattered in all the Nine Realms was his mouth, his tongue, and the way he moved inside of me.

And still it wasn't enough.

I leaned back, pulling him over me. His breath was coming short and fast, and his eyes burned as he watched me. His hand trailed down my stomach, and

I wrapped my fingers around his wrist, pulling it downward, to the place between my legs that ached so in his absence.

"Here." I pressed his fingers to the place he'd discovered. "Oh! Like that!"

His eyes lit as I moaned under him. "You like this?"

"Yes!" I cried.

His smile widened as his fingers slowed, making wide, gentle circles around the apex of my sex. I rippled under his hands, cresting and gasping, but his fingers moved away just a heartbeat before my release, leaving me panting and breathless. I would have begged for more, but under his touch, I'd forgotten how to speak.

"I like this, too," he growled. "I could do this to you forever."

I moaned. My mind was lost in a red haze, and my body felt like I was tumbling, spinning and adrift. He could do this forever, I thought, and I would just float away, my mind lost in an ecstasy of touch.

"But I want to taste you again," he said.

He bent to place his lips on my navel. When the heat of his lips and tongue reached the place his hand had caressed until I'd almost dissolved, the climax I'd been chasing for so long crashed over me, and I fell apart like smoke. I screamed, only vaguely aware that my muscles were seizing, and my hands were clutching at his hair.

Then, as so often happened when I caressed myself in the darkness of our house, tears chased my pleasure. I tried to hide my face against the ground, but a choked cry slipped out of my lips.

"Sol! What is it? What have I done?"

The air suddenly felt cold against my side as he pulled away. I hiccupped another sob into the damp moss. Warm fingers traced my shoulder gingerly, almost as though he was afraid I might break.

"I'm so sorry," he said. "I didn't know—"

"No," I said. "No. It's not you. It's—"

I wiped my eyes and looked at him. His brow had furrowed above his light blue eyes. He looked worried, and more than a little frightened.

"Kiss me," I said.

His frown deepened. "What?"

"Just kiss me."

His eyes widened, and I couldn't wait any longer. I pushed myself off the moss to attack him. He opened his mouth, but my lips were on his, drowning any protest with my tongue. I kissed him hard, digging my fingers into his hair, wrapping my legs around his waist. His cock pulsed beneath me, rigid and urgent. He moaned in surrender.

My tears vanished, evaporating before the rekindled heat of my desire. I wanted him, wanted this demon inside me, wanted him with a thirst so deep and powerful it might never be sated.

"Down," I growled.

Without waiting for him to respond, I shoved his shoulders to the moss. His eyes were still wide and wild, but his thighs tilted upward, thrusting into me. We both cried out as he entered me, my body embracing him, his hips rolling beneath me. I rocked back, closing my eyes. Oh, he felt good!

But it wasn't enough. My legs were wrapped around the most handsome man I'd ever seen, and stars, it wasn't enough.

I was a whore after all.

I leaned over him, opening my eyes slowly. The dappled light made shifting patterns across the taut muscles of his naked chest and the waves of his ember colored hair; his breath came short and fast. His entire body spoke of power contained, of force waiting to be unleashed and, for a heartbeat, I thought of a thundercloud on the horizon.

My hips began to rock without my conscious decision. One moment, I was admiring him, the next I was riding him. Heat flared through my body, sudden and insistent, crashing through me in waves from the place where our bodies joined.

"Oh, Sol," he moaned. His hands grabbed my hips, his grip tightening as my thrusts became more urgent, less rhythmic.

"Demon," I screamed. "My. Demon!"

Deep inside, the coil in my belly grew tighter and tighter. Sweat trickled between my breasts and down the back of my neck; sweat slicked the places where our thighs met. I drove myself into him harder and harder, forcing us together. His fingers dug into my flesh, and his hips met mine, lifting me off the ground.

My climax came like lightning, blinding me, burning me up. A second later, he screamed, and his cock, buried inside me, pulsed with his seed. I collapsed on top of him, breathing him in as our chests rose and fell together. I wondered briefly if I'd ever felt so damned good, and then sleep swallowed me, and I thought of nothing more.

CHAPTER SEVEN

"Sol?"

I frowned as my eyelids fluttered open. The light was all wrong, as if I were outside. But why would I be outside—

"Sol!"

I knew that frantic, urgent voice.

"Ma?" I murmured, forcing my eyes open.

I *was* outside. I blinked, trying to focus in the heavy darkness under the trees, then glanced up. The sky was already a thick indigo. It must be a full hour after sunset; no wonder Ma was calling for me.

I sat up and winced at a deep ache between my legs. Ah, shit. I was completely naked. I dipped my fingers between my legs and felt the thick residue of his seed. Just one more time, the demon had said. I sniffed as my useless tears welled up again.

"Here!" I yelled. "Here, I'm coming!"

"Sol! Hurry! Follow my lantern!"

Ma's voice was pinched and high. Of course. It was almost full dark, and here I was, in the Ironwood. Alone, and naked. A slow shiver ran across my shoulders as a wildly bobbing spot of orange light flashed through the trees.

"I see your lantern," I called. My voice wavered, and I tried to cough out the growing lump in my throat.

One more time.

The orange light of Ma's lantern refracted and then shattered as the tears spilled down my cheeks.

"Sol?" Ma screamed.

She sounded close to panic now. Of course she was. This was the Ironwood in full darkness. Any monster or beast might be here, something that could devour me and leave nothing behind. I ran my hands across the moss until my fingertips snagged the rough fabric of my dress. With a deep sigh, I pulled it over my head.

"Sol!"

I stood and kicked the moss where my demon had lain. Anything at all could be hiding in the thick darkness surrounding me. An end as swift and painless as my father's, perhaps, was waiting for me beneath these trees, ready to take me before King Nøkkyn had his chance.

Something moved behind me, rustling branches just over my shoulder, and I froze. My heart kicked against my chest. I moved across the moss as quickly as I could, my hands raised in front of me, seeking the warm flash of Ma's lantern. Perhaps I wasn't quite ready for my father's end after all.

I stumbled out of the trees, breathless and panting. I hadn't heard another sound, but the hairs across my neck prickled. Ma leaned heavily on her good leg, the lantern at her feet, Da's rusty broadsword clenched in her fists.

"Sol!" she cried. "Oh, thank the stars!"

The orange flame at her feet cast crazy shadows across the contours of her face as I fell into her arms. My entire body trembled.

"I'm so sorry," I said. The words spilled from my lips as choked sobs. "Sorry. So-sorry."

"Shhhh, gentle now. Gentle. Let's get inside."

I reached for the hilt of Da's sword, but Ma shook her head, so I took the lantern instead. Tears rolled down my cheeks, blurring my vision, and my arms and legs trembled as though I really had been running for my life.

"I fell asleep," I stammered, picking my words carefully to avoid outright lies.

"It's fine." Ma moved slowly, limping on her leg and keeping her eyes on the dark shadows under the Ironwood. "It's just fine, Sol."

I shook my head. It was most certainly not fine, but what could either of us do?

OUR NIGHTS GREW COLDER, and the low clouds threatened rain for days. Egren and Jael had yet to return from the Ironwood, and I'd had no sign of my demon in the dozen days since our last meeting. Ma and I were both wound tight as springs, quick to snap at each other and slow to forgive.

I told her this morning I was going to gather mushrooms. She nodded in response. I'd spent half the night staring at the darkness between our roofbeams, trying to think of another excuse to visit the Ironwood. To wait for my brothers, I told myself, although the throbbing ache between my legs told a different story.

The demon said one last time. And I should hope he didn't lie. Demon or not, he'd spilled seed inside me. If that seed took root before King Nøkkyn claimed me, I'd hang, and my family would receive no refund for the damaged goods they'd traded.

I scowled at the gray sky and kicked a rotting stump. It exploded in a very satisfactory manner.

I wasn't just waiting for my brothers, or pining for my demon lover. A bag of beetroot, rags, and an iron pan hung heavily over my shoulder and thudded against my hips with every step. At the Harvest dance last year, I'd overheard two village girls talk of how to convince a new husband that a maidenhead was still intact. Most of it, I gleaned, came down to behavior and blood. Just lie still and look terrified, the older girl said. Afterward, he'll check the sheets for blood.

I didn't remember blood when I gave myself to the demon, although for several days afterward I'd had a strange ache deep inside which filled me with equal parts fear and elation.

Biting my lip, I tried to reign in my wandering mind. I had no doubt I could lie still and look terrified for King Nøkkyn. I was already terrified of him. And the necessary blood, I hoped, could be supplied with beetroot dye.

That wasn't the kind of thing I could count on making in the castle. I knew nothing about my quarters, or what limited freedom I'd be allowed. No, the dye I'd have to make here, now, and carry with me to the castle to spread between my legs before my new owner claimed me.

A raven called. Its sharp voice shattered the still air, and I shivered. Ma said ravens were harbingers of death and, as much as Da insisted they were just birds, I couldn't quite shake that fear.

"Stop being stupid," I hissed under my breath.

I turned north, pushing ferns out of my way as I followed the cheerful chatter of the Lucky river. I was headed for a huge, half submerged rock, where the dark waters of the Lucky pooled and swirled. I planned to build a hidden fire in the lee of that granite boulder. With a little luck and a lot of patience, I'd be able to boil the beetroot juice until it was the color and thickness of blood.

The Lucky came into view, its waters dancing in the sunlight. Little orange insects were hatching across its surface and struggling toward the beams of light that managed to filter down through the pine boughs. They seemed hopelessly vulnerable, so terribly unprepared for what awaited them in the forest. For some reason their halting upward motion made me want to cry.

"Sol."

I jumped, spinning away from the water.

He stood behind the boulder, naked as always, his hair a messy tangle above his pale face. My breath caught in my throat. I stepped toward him without thinking.

"Hello," I said.

He shook his head. Dark circles spread below his haunted eyes. I took another step toward him and realized he was trembling.

"Are you all right?" I asked.

He laughed. It sounded rusty and hollow. "No. No, damn it, I'm not all right."

My heart ached, and I reached for him. His entire body shook when I touched his cool skin.

"Can I help?" I asked.

He sighed and closed his eyes. "It's even worse now," he whispered. "Sol, I...I can't think. I can't sleep. Everything speaks of you, and..."

His voice broke as he met my eyes.

"I need you," he said. "I need you the way I need air. More. Sol, being apart from you, it's like... I feel like I'm dying."

My heart thundered against my chest. I know, I thought. Yes, I know exactly how you feel.

"My poor demon," I whispered.

His head dropped to my shoulders and his chest rose, almost touching my breasts as he inhaled. His hair brushed my collarbone and I shivered, almost afraid to move, lest I shatter the moment.

"May I?" he whispered. His breath sent sparks skidding across my neck and dancing down my back, tightening the soft places deep inside me.

"Please," I sighed, leaning against the solid strength of his chest.

The bag slipped from my shoulders as my leg climbed up his thigh. I pulled up my dress, bunching it around my waist as I spread my legs.

I gave him the comfort of my body.

He entered me quickly, filling me with a shock of pleasure so sudden it made me cry out. Then he was inside me, lifting me, thrusting against me. I staggered backward until my shoulder blades pressed against the cold granite of the enormous boulder, and I arched my back, offering myself to him. His breath hissed against my skin, whispering my name over and over as his hands sank into my hair. He wants me, I realized. He needs me.

Stars, the power of it! To have this beautiful man naked before me, aching for me. I closed my eyes and, for a moment, I was a queen, the most powerful woman in the Nine Realms, with all my subjects spread before me in supplication. I pulled him close, the sweat on our bodies slicking our thighs as our hips moved together.

Pleasure built between us like a fire, starting as a slow flicker and growing larger and larger until it raged beyond control, until he drove my hips into the rock and I dug my heels into his back, screaming for more. It was never enough with him, never, never enough—

My back stiffened, and the world exploded in ecstasy. He groaned above me, shoving me against the boulder as his cock throbbed inside me. His chest fell against mine, squeezing me between the cold granite and the heat of his body. I ran my fingers along the hard planes of his back and up his neck, sinking them into the tangle of his auburn hair.

"Better?" I whispered.

He shook his head against my neck. "No. Sol, I'll wake up tomorrow, and you'll be—"

He froze, then pulled back so suddenly I stumbled forward. His arm caught me before I could fall flat on my face.

"Someone's coming," he whispered.

Panic surged through me, hot and sudden. I held my breath. The Lucky clattered over rocks and hissed past fallen trees. Wind hissed in the high branches and, somewhere far away, another raven called.

"I don't hear anything."

"Shhhhh." He placed a finger on my lips, his eyes going soft as he looked over my shoulder.

I frowned, concentrating. This time I did hear something, like a distant echo. Voices. Two voices, raised in harmony, singing to keep the monsters at bay. My heart leapt.

"Egren and Jael! Oh, it's my brothers!"

"Shhhhhh," he said again. "If we're quiet, they won't hear us."

I frowned at him, wondering if that was meant to be a joke. "They're my brothers. I haven't seen them in over a month."

The demon blinked at me, his eyes clouding with confusion, and tight knot of fear bunched in my stomach. Was the demon going to try to stop me? Was this when he dragged me to Múspell? I stepped away from the cold stone pressing into my back and smoothed my skirt over my thighs.

"They're my family. I'm going to them," I said, defying him.

The demon's brow furrowed into his usual frown. He clenched his fists, looked away, then turned and kissed me softly, his lips just brushing mine. My heart fluttered, and I wondered that such a small, tender kiss should start such a fire inside me.

"Go," he said, staring at the dirt between his toes.

He stepped away from me, his shoulders slumped, and his eyes darkened. I hesitated. He looked so sad and small, standing naked and alone in the filtered light of the Ironwood.

My brothers' voices came again, rising and falling together in song, and my heart ached. They lived. Jael and little Egren had survived. Thank the stars.

When I turned back to collect my bag, my demon had vanished. Soft ferns waved under the trees, every frond unbroken, leaving no hint as to where he'd gone.

"Goodbye," I whispered.

The Lucky River chattered in reply.

CHAPTER EIGHT

The closer I got to my brother's voices, the more frantic and rushed they sounded. A heavy knot of worry settled on my chest as I rushed toward their echoing refrains. They were singing an old logging song, but they were singing it too quickly, almost breathlessly, as if they were running.

Had there been a problem? An accident?

I tried to ignore the tightening in my chest. I could hear both voices singing, Jael's deep baritone and Egren's lighter, younger tenor, but that didn't mean they were both unharmed. Egren's little body flashed through my mind, my baby brother climbing high into the purple oaks, a shimmering blade tucked under his arm.

"Egren!" I yelled. "Jael!"

The singing paused.

"Sol?" Jael's call echoed back to me, ringing through the tree trunks.

My heart leapt, and I raced through the forest, ignoring the little branches that pulled at my clothes and tangled my hair. Several paces later, I crashed through ferns as high as my shoulders and almost plowed into Jael's broad chest.

"Sol!" he cried.

He blinked at me for a moment before shrugging off the sledge's shoulder harness and wrapping me in his enormous arms. He crushed me to his chest, and for a heartbeat I was so strongly reminded of my father that it made my heart ache with a vast, echoing loneliness.

"By the stars, Sol, what are you doing here?"

He pulled back, holding me at arm's length, and I saw the tight lines around his mouth, the tense knot of his shoulders. Beside him, Egren's little upturned face was pale, his eyes wide. But the sledge was loaded with fine, straight purple oak limbs; they should have been joyful, not terrified.

"What's wrong?" I asked.

"Shhhh. Sing." Jael's eyes jumped from me to the darkness of the forest, and immediately he and Egren began the third refrain. It was Da's song, the one he always told us was magical. To keep the monsters of Ironwood at bay.

My poor brothers. They had no idea I was under the protection of a demon, a protection I was certain extended to them.

"We're fine," I said. "You don't need to worry. My lov—"

A branch snapped in the woods behind us, and I clamped my mouth shut. Stars, what had I been about to say?

Jael's hand tightened on my shoulder, and I winced.

"Sing," he hissed.

I nodded. "From the darkness comes the light," I sang, joining the chorus. "From our softness comes our strength."

"From the darkness comes the light," Jael echoed, gesturing to Egren.

Egren moved beside him, linking hands with Jael. They both stared at me.

"From the black earth grows the sun-wheat," they sang.

"From the ashes springs the fire," I added.

Jael nodded as he pulled the harness back onto his shoulders. The thick mud behind him squelched as the sledge slid reluctantly forward.

"So from the darkness," we sang together, "comes the light."

I followed Egren and Jael, looking back over my shoulder. The branches swayed behind us, but whether it was our motion or the movement of some unseen figure making them dance, I could not have said.

"SOL GOES INTO THOSE woods."

I jolted awake at Ma's voice. I'd been dozing by the fire, my arms wrapped around Egren's chest. He used to sleep with me as a baby. Now, I could scarcely believe his lanky little body belonged to the same boy I'd once nuzzled as an infant. Egren had gone from a chubby, cheerful toddler to a tall, serious child. It was as if my father's death had brought old age to his young frame like frost settling on the crops, shriveling and blackening them.

Jael was all smiles once we emerged from the Ironwood, and he refused to answer my questions about what had them both so scared. It was just as well,

I slowly realized, as I could scarcely explain my similar insistence that we had nothing to fear.

They had found a beautiful purple oak, he recounted over the dinner table. Egren limbed the top branches, Jael cut them into usable lumber, and now the tree was ready to fell. With any luck, Jael said, they would be able to load three or four sledge loads of lumber before the snow fell. But I noted the tightness in his shoulders as he spoke, and the hard glint in his eyes. Something had happened to them in the shadows of the Ironwood. Something my brothers refused to mention at the dinner table, or after. But now the fire was low, and Jael had every reason to think I was sleeping.

"I know," Jael said, his voice low and thick in the darkness of our cabin. "What in the Nine Realms was Sol doing so deep in the Ironwood?"

Ma made a thick noise deep in her throat. "Leave her be. She's little enough time to enjoy her freedom."

"But it's not safe, Ma," Jael pressed. "I saw the tracks myself. They were longer than my forearm. And they were fresh."

"On the old road?"

"And the new. And the path by the Lucky as well."

Ma hissed through her teeth.

"The tracks are on all the trails," Jael said, dropping his voice. "That monster Fenris is circling this house."

I opened my eyes slowly, focusing on the flickering embers of the fire. Egren sighed in his sleep.

"But, what can we do?" Ma said.

Jael grunted. The bench creaked beneath him as he leaned back. "There's not a damn thing we can do. It's not like we have the money to move, is it? And I've no wish to be sold into slavery like Sol."

"Hush! You know she had little enough choice. And just imagine the mess we'd be in if she'd refused!"

Jael sighed. "Stars. I don't like this any more than you do."

They both fell silent. A small flame leapt from the ashes, reached for the darkness of the chimney, and then fell back, extinguished by its own desire.

"I can go see the witch-lady in the morning to beg some protection," Jael said. "And we need to keep Sol close."

I bit my lip, trying to keep my breathing even while my heart thundered against my ribs. I'd seen no tracks, nor any sign of Fenris the monster wolf. But I didn't doubt my brother's words. We'd both been raised in the shadows of the Ironwood. Da claimed he'd once seen the Light-elves a-hunting in the deep forest, and Ma had seen the sprites. As a child, once, Jael had taken me into the forest to show me the tracks of a were-bear.

And hadn't I taken a demon lover from Múspell in the darkness of the Ironwood?

Tears bit behind my lids. My demon wanted me to call him Fenris, the silly thing. But if he met the real Fenris, the monster wolf who stood as tall as the trees, my little demon wouldn't stand a chance. His muscular, naked body filled my mind, his delicate fingers and burning, pale eyes. He was strong, and I didn't doubt he was brave, but against the monster of the Ironwood?

I pictured his beautiful body broken, pierced by teeth bigger than broadswords, and I had to feign a coughing fit to hide the sob that choked me.

CHAPTER NINE

Fear kept me awake.

Fear, and the image of my lover's beautiful body, bloodied, broken, and flung to the forest floor. Ma and Jael talked some time longer, speculating about what the family would need to survive the winter and how much they could spare to give the witch-woman in exchange for protection from the Fenris-wolf. When they said there would only be three mouths to feed that winter, my gut twisted into a tight, angry knot. They wouldn't need to worry about me when the snow fell; I'd be a pampered whore in King Nøkkyn's harem come winter. My mouth tasted bitter as I struggled to keep my breathing level and even, as though I were still asleep.

Finally, the benches creaked and scraped as Ma and Jael lay down in their sleeping furs. I waited and waited, watching the fire's embers die slowly, one by one, and listening to the steady hiss of their breathing. Only when the cottage was entirely dark did I dare to ease my arm out from under Egren's head and come to my feet.

Enough moonlight fell through the doorframe to reveal the huddled shapes of my mother and brothers curled on the floor. Jael was snoring, the rough timbre of his breathing so like my Da it almost pained me to listen. My heart raced as I backed away from their prone figures, treading lightly and hardly daring to breathe.

It was cold when I stepped through the door. The swollen moon hung low over the trees of the Ironwood, bathing our dooryard and kitchen garden in an odd, pale light which made the whole world look like it was underwater. I marveled that the yard I'd known all my life could look so strange.

Twenty steps took me to the fringe of Ironwood. I shivered, pulling my arms around my thin dress. I'd never dared to go into the Ironwood at night. No one traveled through the Ironwood at night. Even my brothers and father, when they cut their purple oaks, lit fires and kept a watch all night.

It was madness to enter the Ironwood in the dark.

I closed my eyes and saw his beautiful body, my demon lover, broken and bleeding from the fangs of the Fenris-wolf. Swallowing hard, I stepped under the trees.

The forest was strange in the pale glimmer of moonlight, drained of color and filled with unfamiliar noises. Distance was hard to judge. By the time I reached the banks of the Lucky, I felt I'd been walking for hours. But, when I stumbled upon the boulder where Fenris and I'd made love that morning, I couldn't believe I'd already traveled so far.

The water was filled with moonlight, sparkling and chattering. Nightbirds called to one another above my head, their voices loud and shrill. Soft, dark shapes swirled in the air, dipping to the surface of the water, then sweeping high above my head. It was strangely beautiful, like I'd trespassed into another world to watch something meant for other eyes.

"Hello?" I whispered.

My voice bounced strangely off the rocks, the water, the trees. The whisper that returned to me was a distance echo, like it had been wrapped in thick linen and dropped down a well.

"Demon?" I said, raising my voice. "Are you here?"

The birds fell silent. Even the dark, swooping shapes above the water vanished. I felt the hairs along the back of my neck prickle, and I turned, staring into the darkness. Stars, I should have brought my father's broadsword. Or at least a knife.

"F-Fenris?" I whispered.

My mouth had gone horribly dry. I had trouble even forming the ridiculous name my demon lover had adopted. Too late, I realized what cursed luck it must be to whisper the name of the monster Fenris-wolf in the darkness of the Ironwood.

"Sol?"

I jumped and spun. My demon emerged from behind the deep shadows of the boulder, naked as always, the shine of the moonlight making him pale and even more unearthly than usual.

"Oh, stars!" I fell against him, running my hands along his chest as if seeking reassurance that he was whole and unharmed.

"You missed me?" he asked.

I turned to see the hint of a smile tugging at the corner of his mouth. He looked like he was begging for a kiss; I was only too happy to oblige. I sank into him, twining my fingers in his hair as our tongues embraced.

I had missed him, damn it. It had only been an afternoon, and I'd missed him terribly. He dropped his hands to my thighs, pulling at the fabric of my dress.

"Wait," I gasped.

His smile crumpled into a frown. "What's wrong?"

"I need to warn you. My brothers, they saw—"

I hesitated. Here, with my lover's strong arms wrapped around my waist and the heat of his erection pressing into my stomach, Jael's fears suddenly seemed insignificant.

"Tracks," I whispered. "Monster's tracks. Demon, there are dangers in the Ironwood—"

His chest shook against mine. A moment later, his laughter poured over the Lucky, filling the spaces between the trees.

"Oh, Sol! Did you walk the Ironwood at night to warn me of its dangers?"

I flushed. Coming from his mouth, my actions seemed ridiculous. Stupid, even.

"I was scared." My voice sounded small against the darkness. "I kept thinking of you hurt, or—" I choked. I couldn't bring myself to say it.

He kissed me, and my fear vanished, sublimated by the slowly spreading burn of arousal. When we pulled apart, he met my gaze with an oddly serious expression.

"I believe you're the first person to ever express concern for my safety," he said. His voice was so low, it was almost swallowed by the hiss and chatter of water over stones.

I laughed at the absurdity of that statement. Any woman who saw his handsome face and beautiful body would fall in love with him. There had to be dozens of maidens in the fringes of the Ironwood who fretted over his safety. My heart twisted painfully, and I pulled back to stare at the muscles of his chest in an attempt to banish the nightmare image of his beautiful body lying broken and bloody among the leaves of the forest floor. He touched my chin, tilting my head until our eyes met. His blue eyes shone in the moonlight like an animal's.

"I'm not a demon," he said.

I sighed. It seemed pointless to argue this now.

"Do you live here? In the Ironwood?" I asked. I couldn't quite keep the tremble from my voice.

"Of course."

"Then you have to be careful! Please! It's dangerous!"

His soft lips curved into a smile. "Are you saying I shouldn't run into the Ironwood at night? Alone?"

I felt blood rush to my cheeks. "Just...be careful."

"Beautiful Sol. There's nothing in the Ironwood that could harm Fenris."

I snorted. "Well, there's the actual Fenris, for one. The monster wolf. And there are bears, even if they aren't were-bears, they're dangerous. And the Light-elves come hunting here, they don't much care what they catch—"

His hips started moving against mine in a very distracting way, and my breath caught in my throat. When he bent to put his lips along the curve of my throat, my litany of monsters evaporated like the morning fog.

"Sol," he hissed against my skin. "I promise you, I will tread the wild paths of the Ironwood with the utmost care."

A moan slipped from my lips. His touch sent sparks skidding across my skin, and the rough fabric of my dress suddenly felt too hot, too confining. I ached for the press of his muscles against mine, the heat of our bodies combined.

"Fenris," I whispered. "I did miss you."

His lips were on mine before I could say more. He wrapped his hands around my thighs, shoving my dress up to my waist. Even that was too much fabric, too great a barrier between our bodies. I pulled away from the heat of his arms long enough to yank the threadbare dress over my head and toss it into the darkness.

He was on me as soon as the dress vanished, the hard muscles of his chest pressed against my breasts until my shoulders met the cold grit of the massive boulder embedded in the riverbank. His breath spread against my neck, flooding my body with heat, slicking my thighs, making me burn.

"I missed you," he growled against my neck. "It wasn't enough. It's never enough."

I opened my mouth to say yes, it's never enough, but his lips dropped to my chest, and I could only gasp as his tongue ran over the hard jut of my nipple.

His soft mouth engulfed my breast and I gasped, digging my shoulders into the rock, arching my back, granting him access to everything, all of me.

He fell to his knees, pulling my leg over his shoulder. Overhead, the brilliant stars spun through the trees as his mouth set my body aflame. My demon devoured me, his tongue entering me over and over, his lips and teeth caressing the hard nub at the apex of my sex until the dancing stars, the hard rock under my naked back, the trees of the Ironwood, all whirled and burned and fell away to nothingness. He devoured me until I lost myself, drowning in the waves of his ecstasy. I dug my fingers into his hair and screamed his name, as if I were daring the monsters of the forest to show themselves.

His body shifted beneath me, and I struggled to focus. My climax had left me trembling, with my vision blurred and my skin so sensitive it almost burned. The demon's arms wrapped around my waist, then my shoulders, and he guided me to the soft, cool moss along the Lucky's bank. He ran his lips over me, laying a trail of kisses along my collarbone and up the side of my neck. My body sang with pleasure; his touch was like a flame licking my skin, burning away everything but joy. It was almost too much to take. I moaned and writhed below him.

"Oh, my Sol!" He spread my legs as he covered my body with his.

He entered me, pressing my hips into the moss, and suddenly his caresses went from too much to not nearly enough. My body cried out for him, demanding to be filled.

"More," I panted. "More, damn it!"

His lips twisted into a smile. The moonlight painted his handsome face in pale shades of gray.

"Anything you desire," he said in a rasp as rough as the granite boulder.

His hips moved against mine in a slow circle. He dropped his hand and pressed his fingers against my sex, caressing the spot he first discovered. My words faded into animal gasps, and I rocked back, closing my eyes. I hadn't realized I could die more than once in a night, that I could fall apart, be pulled back together, and then fall apart again. I dissolved under those slender hips, screaming his name, grabbing at his hair and shoulders, tearing the moss beneath my toes. When his cries finally joined mine and his stiff cock pulsed deep inside me, I was no longer certain where his body ended and my own began.

"SOL?"

I sighed, shifting sleepily in my demon's arms. It felt so good to lie against the warmth of his body, with his rich, forest scent wrapping me like a blanket. His hair tickled the back of my neck as he leaned over me.

My eyes opened, and I turned to smile at him. His bright eyes shone brighter than the sky.

"My beautiful Sol. Morning approaches. Will you be missed?"

A jolt shot through my chest, and I forced myself to sit up. Yes, the sky was unmistakably lighter now, with only a handful of scattered stars twinkling across the indigo of early morning.

"Shit!" I scrambled to my knees, scanning the moss for my clothes.

The pale fabric of my dress had been gracefully draped across the boulder. Blood rushed to my cheeks as I realized my demon must have picked it up and hung it over the rock to keep it from getting wet with dew. I imagined him moving away from my sleeping body to care for my clothes, and a new, entirely uncomfortable thought flared in the depths of my mind.

King Nøkkyn.

I should tell him, I realized as my empty stomach shifted uneasily. I should tell him my body does not belong to me, that less than two months remain before I'm dragged to the castle's harems.

Fenris stood and picked up my dress, shaking it once. He smiled shyly as he handed it to me. A great wave of shame and loneliness swept through me, more powerful than the currents of the Körmt river. I hoped it was dark enough to hide the tears welling behind my eyelids.

"Shall I walk you home?" he asked. "I've heard the Ironwood can be dangerous."

I tried to smile at his little joke. "Please."

The morning birds were already calling to each other high in the pines of the Ironwood when I finally stepped across the lintel of our house, careful not to disturb the sleeping bodies sprawled across the floor. Ma stirred in her sleep as I pulled the wooden door closed but, thank the stars, Jael was silent. Egren had twisted in his sleep, so his bare little toes almost touched the cold hearth. I pulled the fur over him again and settled beside him quietly as I could manage. When I wrapped my arms around my cold, aching chest, I realized I could still smell my demon lover Fenris on my hands and hair. I closed my eyes, pretending his arms still encircled me, and let myself drift into an uneasy sleep.

CHAPTER TEN

"But what do you eat?" I insisted.

Fenris and I lay stretched out on the moss along the Lucky, my clothes draped over the now familiar boulder, and the pitiful results of my half-hearted attempt to collect mushrooms sitting neglected in the shade of a massive pine. His sweat still covered my body, and his seed streaked my thighs.

Jael had tried to stop me this morning. Chopping the purple oak Jael and Egan had pulled out of the Ironwood, and then harvesting and packing the winter potatoes, had kept us all busy for nearly a week. I hadn't seen Fenris during that time, and I'd missed him with a fierce desperation that defied all logic. This morning, when the first golden streaks of dawn stretched across the pale sky, I grabbed a harvesting basket and leapt out the door, but Jael stepped in front of me, his arms crossed over his chest.

"Where do you think you're going?" he'd said.

My heart rattled in my chest as I lifted the basket and tried to smile innocently. "To collect mushrooms. I saw some golden orbs last week."

Jael shook his head. "Sol, it's too dangerous. You need to stay where we can see you."

My gut knotted as my breath caught in my throat. Where he could see me? Stars, no! My days of freedom were slipping through my fingers like water, and I wanted to spend the last of them with my legs wrapped around my demon lover, trying to memorize the way his skin felt against mine, the rasp of his breath against my ear, the sweet ecstasy of his body. I couldn't stay here, in the cage of this cottage. Not while Fenris waited in the shadows of the Ironwood.

I opened my mouth to beg, or to cry, but Ma spoke for me.

"Jael," she said from behind us, "let her go."

Jael's shoulders slumped as he looked past me into the darkness of the house. "But, Ma—"

"Just let her go," she said. "Sol has little enough time to enjoy her solitude."

I turned to smile at Ma, trying to ignore the worry lines creased across her forehead. My chest twisted with guilt as I sprinted into the darkness of the Ironwood, but it was nothing compared to the aching need surging through the rest of my body. I burned for Fenris. When held against that raging fire, the guilt and shame I felt at my deception melted into a dull, uncomfortable throb, like a week-old bruise. Easy enough to ignore.

Fenris smiled at me as the Lucky sang behind him. "What do you mean, what do I eat?"

"If you live alone in the Ironwood, then what in the Nine Realms do you eat?"

My fingers made a lazy circle in his auburn curls. I'd been thinking about him constantly. Could he possibly survive on squirrels and mushrooms in the forest?

"There's plenty to eat in the Ironwood," he said. "Why? Is my Sol hungry?"

I shook my head, but my stomach pinched painfully at the word *hungry*. It was going to be a long winter for my mother and brothers. I tried not to make it worse by eating their potatoes.

"I just wonder how you survive out here by yourself."

He sighed, rolling onto his back. "Mostly deer, if you must know. And bread."

I laughed before I could stop myself. "Bread? In the middle of the Ironwood? What, you're a baker?"

His pale, sparkling eyes met mine. "I don't bake it myself."

"So you go into the village, naked as the day you were born, and buy a few loaves of bread every month?"

His grin widened. "Of course not. But you won't believe me if I tell you."

"I don't believe most of the things you tell me."

He shrugged, but the light in his eyes dimmed, and I regretted my words. Even if they were true.

"Tell me," I said.

"I have a friend who brings me bread and mead every full moon."

My heart gave a kick at that. Another woman, I was sure of it. And why not? Wasn't I promised to King Nøkkyn, a little detail I'd somehow not yet managed to share with him? Why shouldn't he have multiple lovers?

"It's not like that," he said, softly.

I turned away, disturbed he'd been able to read me so easily.

"Týr," he said. "A great warrior of the Æsir. He's my friend. My very good friend. He brings me bread and mead from Asgard."

I snorted. "That's ridiculous. The Æsir never come to the Ironwood."

Fenris's hands traced the curve of my back, dropping to the swell of my hips. I still didn't turn around. Why would he tell me something impossible? Why not admit a woman brought him food?

"Týr comes every month," he said. His voice was low and rough. My skin prickled with heat as his lips moved along my neck. "I'll prove it to you."

I closed my eyes and let him kiss me. What did it matter if he told outrageous stories to match his ridiculous name? In another month I'd be gone to the cold, dark towers of Nøkkyn's fortress, and this beautiful, impossible demon who called himself Fenris would be nothing but a memory. I willed the tears away and rolled onto my back.

His eyes widened at the sight of my breasts, as they always did, and I wondered that it should give me so much pleasure to watch him admire my body.

"More," I said. "I want more."

Still smiling, he gave me what I wanted.

IT WAS ANOTHER TWO days before I could slip into the Ironwood again. Jael and Egen were busy preparing to return to their purple oak to harvest as much as they could before the snows came, and it took all of us to cook and pack for them. The clouds hung heavy as dawn broke that morning, full of rain and almost dragging along the tops of the Ironwood's trees.

"We won't be leaving today," Jael said, with a sigh.

My heart leapt. "You won't be needing me, then," I said, trying to keep the edge of excitement out of my voice.

Ma smiled at me. "Yes, Sol, you can run off to the woods."

Jael frowned. "What in the Nine Realms do you do in there, anyway?"

"Nothing!" I said, far too quickly to be convincing.

"Jael. Let her be," Ma said. "You loved the woods too, as a child."

Jael snorted. "Sol's hardly a child. I'd think she'd be a bit more help around here than leaving for the entire day and coming back with a half dozen shriveled little mushrooms."

I bit my lip as the familiar sting of guilt and shame chased each other through my gut. "I haven't seen anything dangerous in the woods," I said, quite honestly. "Not even a bear track, I swear it on the stars."

"But I have," Jael said in a cold, low voice.

Ma leaned across the table and rested her hand on Jael's arm. "Let her go. Sol is doing quite enough for the family."

I shivered at that, and my empty stomach lurched. I couldn't help counting the days, now. It had been twenty seven yesterday. Now it was twenty six.

Twenty six days until King Nøkkyn claimed me.

Jael sighed and shook his head. "Fine. Just, please, be safe. Stay where we can hear you if you scream."

"Of course," I said, nodding cheerfully as I backed out the door.

I sure as hell wasn't going to stay where they could hear me.

And I was planning on screaming.

CHAPTER ELEVEN

My bare feet raced over the cold moss and pine duff of the Ironwood. I didn't even bring a gathering basket this time; there was no need to pretend I was doing anything other than escaping, running into the woods to enjoy my last days of freedom. The slow drizzle of cold rain fell softly beneath the trees and, although my thin dress was soon soaked through, I didn't feel cold.

I followed the Lucky's gentle meanders through a small birch grove and into the shadows of the enormous, ancient pines. The forest smelled of gentle decay, rainwater, and the tang of pine tannins. My breath quickened when I saw our boulder ahead, looming over a sharp bend in the Lucky's murmuring waters. Fenris had been at that rock the last time I'd seen him, his muscular, naked body resting again the moss-dappled stone, almost as though he'd taken to spending all his time along the Lucky River, waiting for me.

My heart beat a little faster at that pleasant fantasy.

I frowned as I stepped from the shadows into the thick, gray drizzle. Fenris wasn't waiting for me, but there was something resting atop our rock. I bit my lip and edged closer. It was a small, dark shape, almost like a river stone. I was close enough to touch it when I finally recognized what it was.

Bread.

A small, round loaf of dark bread waited for me on our rock. My stomach rumbled in anticipation, and my hands trembled when I reached for it, closing my cold fingers around the rasp of its thick crust. I brought it to my nose, breathing deeply. Oh, it was sweet rye! My mouth ached as it watered, and my fingers traced the surface.

Someone had already taken a knife to this loaf. I turned the bread over in my hands, and my vision blurred with a sudden rush of tears. A small, dark heart had been cut in the center of the bread.

My chest clenched until it almost hurt to breathe. Yes, I'd kissed boys in the village before. I'd even let Bryn run his hands up my thighs and press his stiff cock into my stomach as we danced. But none of those boys had ever given me so much as a ribbon for my hair.

"Oh, Fenris," I whispered as my fingers traced the heart. I pictured him holding a sharp, silver knife, smiling as he imagined my reaction to the sweet little gesture.

I pulled off a piece of the bread and brought it to my lips. My mouth flooded with the taste; sweet, rich, and deep. Oh, stars! I took another bite and closed my eyes, carried away by the flavor. Bread! An entire loaf, and just for me!

I tried to eat it slowly, to truly savor the experience, but the bread was gone far too soon, and I found myself blinking in the light rain, staring at my own empty hands. My lips and mouth still held the flavor, and too late I wished I'd saved just a crust to smell as I walked back home.

With a hot rush of guilt, it occurred to me that I should have brought the entire loaf home and shared it with my mother and brothers. Of course, that could have led to uncomfortable questions—

"Did you like it?"

I spun to see Fenris standing behind me, a smile on his lips.

"Oh! Fenris!" I flung myself into his arms, burying my face in his neck.

"Did you get my message?" he asked.

I nodded, not trusting myself to speak.

"That's not all. Watch."

He stepped behind a tree and emerged with his hands full. A huge leather water skin was tucked under one arm, and in the other—

"A drinking horn?" I asked, unbelieving. "You have a drinking horn?"

"Of course." He grinned. "How else would you drink mead?"

"Mead?" I couldn't quite keep the disbelief out of my voice.

I'd heard of mead, of course, in Bard Sturlinsen's stories and songs, but I'd never actually seen it. Only kings and the Æsir and Vanir of Asgard drank mead. The men in our village drank fermented apple cider, or a salty wheat beer Da said tasted like horse sweat. And they drank from wooden or ceramic steins, often emblazoned with their names and proudly displayed above the hearth fire in the inn. None of them had anything as elegant as a drinking horn.

"From my friend Týr," Fenris said with unmistakable pride. "I told you I'd prove it."

My lip curled. "Right. Your friend the Æsir."

Fenris raised an eyebrow at me. Then he balanced the water skin against our rock and turned the tap. A light, golden liquid flowed into the pale drinking horn.

"For my lady Sol of the Ironwood," he said, handing me the horn. "The finest mead in the Nine Realms."

I hesitated, then took the drinking horn with both hands. It was long, and heavier than I expected. Its smooth surface was streaked with gold and black; even to my untrained eyes, it looked ancient. A silver band with some sort of writing ringed the top.

"What is this?" I said, running a finger over the runes. "Is it a spell? Are you enchanting me, demon?"

He smiled. "It says, *Friend of the Æsir*. That's all."

I sniffed the liquid, which appeared to be bubbling faintly. It smelled pleasant enough, a bit like honey and a bit like the haze of spilled beer that hovered around the drinking tents at the Midsummer's Festival. Eyeing the length of the horn, I tried to recall everything I'd ever heard about mead. The most important thing seemed to be draining the entire horn. Failure to do so was a grave offense in all the Sturlinsen stories.

I took a deep breath and brought the horn to my lips. The mead was almost pleasant, although it stung a bit as it slid down my throat. I choked when I raised the horn further, and liquid spilled from the corners of my mouth to run down my cheeks. My eyes swam with tears but, by the stars, I could do this. I would do this.

Gasping, I dropped the horn to the grass. Empty! Finally, it was empty! My body flushed with heat, and my head spun strangely, as though I'd whirled and whirled in circles until I could barely stand.

Fenris stared at me with very wide eyes.

"That's a lot of mead," he stammered.

I wiped my lips. "It drinks good."

I giggled at my own words, then giggled again at his silly, serious expression. Oh, stars, he was handsome! I moved to kiss him, stumbled, and fell against his naked chest. I raised myself on my toes, seeking his soft lips.

"Are you okay?" he asked, pulling back.

"Mmmm-hmmm," I purred. "Kiss me."

He did. I wrapped my arms around his chest, trying to keep my balance as the forest spun and shifted under my feet. His lips against mine were pure bliss. They were the most important thing in the Nine Realms. They were the only thing in the Nine Realms. I closed my eyes as my entire being focused on his touch, his lips.

We danced like that for a long time, our mouths pressed together, our kiss the most important, essential thing in the universe. I felt so damned good, warm and soft around the edges, as though his mead had banished all the unpleasantness from life.

His manhood twitched against my thighs, swelling and hardening. I moved again, seeking his heat, but my feet slipped on the moss and I fell to the side, breaking our kiss. His hand grabbed my elbow.

"Sol, I should have warned you. Mead can go to your head."

I giggled again. Was he always so serious?

"My head is good, sexy demon," I said, although my words came out sounding a little fuzzy. My gaze slid from his face to the drinking horn on the ground.

"Drain, drain, drain your horn," I sang, remembering some of the doggerel the men chanted under the Midsummer's Festival drinking tent. "Drain it while it's thick." I giggled again, then turned to Fenris. "Can you drain it?"

His eyebrows raised. "Can I what?"

I let my eyes slide down the length of his lean, naked body. The Midsummer drinking song made it sound like a test of manhood to drain a whole horn.

"I mean, if I can drain the horn, I'm sure a demon of Múspell can do the same..."

"I'm not a demon," he muttered.

"Oh, I know! You're not a demon. You're the mighty Fenris, great monster of the Ironwood. Taller than a stallion, that Fenris. Fiercer than a were-bear."

I stepped back and cocked my head to look at him, but the effect was ruined somewhat by a hiccup slipping from my lips. A dark expression halfway between a smile and a scowl crossed Fenris's lips.

"You don't think I can drain a single horn of mead?" He shook his head. "I guess you really don't know me."

That stung.

"So, prove it," I pushed. "If you're so great, then show me!"

He sighed, then knelt to the grass and picked up the horn. I watched as he turned the tap to fill the horn.

"All the way," I insisted. "Full as mine."

He raised an eyebrow as he showed me the horn. Light golden liquid swirled and effervesced, coming all the way to the pale rim. I nodded, trying to look as serious as he did, although I couldn't seem to stop smiling.

He raised the horn to his lips and tilted his head back. Not quite as tall as a stallion, my demon, but he was a good head taller than me, with a body of lean, hard muscle. His dark, fiery hair cascaded down his back as his neck moved. A trickle of mead leaked from the side of his mouth. I wanted to lick it.

"There!" he shouted as he dropped the horn, his cheeks flushed with triumph.

A pang of regret lanced through my chest as he wiped the mead from his cheek.

"Very nice." I tried to whistle but it came out funny.

He shrugged. "It's not hard. Just open your throat and breath through your nose."

"Open your throat and breath through your nose," I repeated.

Just like that, I wanted to do it again. I wanted to show him that I could drain a horn of mead as well as he could. Maybe I could be a friend to the Æsir, too.

Or, shit, maybe I could be one of the Æsir. Everyone knew Loki the Liesmith was born in the slums of Útgarðar, not so far from the dark fringe of the Ironwood. And now he was one of them, living in Asgard and traveling the Nine Realms with his sworn blood-brother Óðinn.

"Pour me another one," I said.

Fenris shook his head. "No. Sol, these days one is enough to make even my head spin."

I ran my fingers along his neck and rubbed my body against his. "Come on. I want to do it again."

His back arched, but his arms wrapped around my waist. "That much mead is not a good idea."

I giggled at that. I wouldn't call anything we'd done together an especially good idea.

"Please," I pleaded. "Now that you've shown me how it's done. Please. Let me. I wanna show you I can."

Fenris glanced at the somewhat deflated water skin, frowning. The woods seemed to pulse and sway around him.

"Are you denying me?" I said, pouting at him. "The mighty Fenris of Ironwood has never denied me anything before."

He sighed heavily. "Fine. But just a few more sips. By the Realms, don't drain the entire thing."

"But I can," I insisted. "I can drain a horn just like Thor the Thunderer."

Fenris raised an eyebrow as he held the ivory drinking horn to the tap. "You are hardly Thor, little Sol of the Ironwood."

Oh, that did it. I was suddenly filled with the deep, unquenchable need to prove him wrong, to prove them all wrong. It didn't matter that I was the daughter of slaves and soon to be Nøkkyn's whore, stars damn it. I'd show my arrogant, beautiful lover I could drain his stupid horn just as well as his damned friend the Æsir.

I grabbed the horn from his hand and brought it to my mouth. The first splash through my lips tasted good, but taste was not my concern. I tilted my head back, closing my eyes and opening my throat. The ground under my feet tilted alarmingly, but I ignored it. My entire being focused on draining the horn, proving I could take it all in. The world spun around me.

My gut shifted in an odd way as the mead burned its way down my body. My legs flashed with heat before going numb. I dared a quick breath through my nose and forced myself to keep swallowing. The mead didn't taste good anymore; it snatched at my throat and stomach lining.

Another breath and I dared to crack open my eyes. I could see the distant tip of the drinking horn raised in front of my face. Almost there. Now it felt like I was swallowing gravel, but still, I opened my throat and took it all in.

My eyes widened as the bottom of the horn suddenly appeared, draining all at once. I gasped for air, pulled the empty horn from my lips, and staggered back. The ground rose very suddenly to collide with my rear, but I didn't feel a thing.

"I did it," I said. My lips felt numb.

Fenris's frowning face swam into view above me. There seemed to be two of him. Or possibly three. "Stars! Sol, are you all right?"

I tried to snort. Of course I was all right. I was better than all right. I was like Thor, damn it. I could drain a horn like one of the Æsir. I could be one of the Æsir!

"Sol?"

Fenris came closer. He was swaying very strangely from side to side, and his brow was contorted into his usual frown.

He was always so damned serious. I opened my mouth to tell him I was just fine, I was, in fact, feeling great, when something deep inside my stomach lurched violently. A hot jet of vomit poured from my lips, hitting Fenris's naked chest.

"Shit," he yelped.

I gasped in shame and clasped my fingers over my mouth, then choked as another wave of hot mead welled up inside me. It wrenched my mouth open, covering my fingers and running down my dress. The forest dissolved in hot, angry tears.

"Sol, I'm sorry," Fenris said from the red haze that filled my vision. "I'm so sorry."

I was dimly aware of Fenris's hands on my shoulders, tilting me to my side as I retched and retched, my body seizing and spasming, far beyond my control. Gagging and sobbing as my stomach turned itself inside out, I pressed my cheek against the moss of the forest floor and closed my eyes, waiting for it to be over.

CHAPTER TWELVE

"Sol?"

Somewhere beyond the throbbing agony in my head and the churning acid in my stomach, the Lucky River was laughing. And someone was shaking my shoulder. Something wet and cool pressed against my forehead. I reached for it and found a soft strip of moss.

"Oh, Sol. I'm so sorry."

I turned toward his voice, even though the motion sent a hot bolt of pain through my skull. Fenris lay next to me, close enough to touch, his blue eyes wide. A sudden wave of shame and embarrassment swept over me, making the back of my throat taste bitter. I closed my eyes to block out his beautiful visage.

It was no good. Gentle fingers traced the curve of my cheek.

"I cleaned your dress," he whispered. "I-I didn't want to wake you up, but it's almost dark."

Almost dark? I forced myself to sit up, then groaned at the painful throb in my temples. The headache was so bad I could almost ignore the treacherous rumblings in my gut. Fenris's arm wrapped around my shoulders.

"I'm sorry," he said. "I wasn't thinking. It was stupid of me to try to prove Týr is my friend—"

"Shut up," I hissed.

He fell silent. Somehow, that only made me feel worse.

Fenris helped me stagger to my feet. My dress pressed against my breasts and stomach, the damp fabric clinging to my skin. He must have washed it while I lay on the moss, dead to the world. He must have washed himself off, too. I gritted my teeth at the vivid memory of my vomit splattering his bare chest. I'd heard mead dulled memories, but I suspected I was going to be stuck with that horrible image for the rest of my life.

Fenris offered me his arm without speaking. I tried to think of something to say, anything to erase the humiliation of what I'd just done, but every time

I opened my mouth, the words refused to come. We walked through the Iron-wood in silence.

As the mist-shrouded herb garden of our house came into view, I realized with a fresh wave of nausea that there were many other things I should tell Fenris. About King Nøkkyn. And about the Harvest Festival, the day my freedom would end.

Fenris cleared his throat. "Sol—"

I winced. He was whispering, but his voice still pounded at my temples.

"Don't," I said. "Just...don't."

He looked like he might actually cry. It was a horrible expression, and I couldn't bear it on his handsome face.

I turned and limped through the mist without a backward glance.

Ma, Jael, and Egren all turned to stare at me when I stumbled through the door. They were working together on the heavy towing strap for Jael's sled, oiling the leather and patching the holes. They were doing, I realized, exactly what I should have been doing. My stomach lurched, and I ground my teeth together, fighting the rising wave of mead in my gut. A small fire crackled on the hearth, keeping the chill of the fog away; to me it felt too bright, and far too hot.

"I'm not feeling well," I stammered.

I grabbed a sleeping fur and yanked it under the table. Ignoring their concerned faces, I pulled the furs over my head and let darkness swallow me.

THIRST WOKE ME.

My entire body ached, and my throat burned for water. The hearth fire had died down, until it was just a dim flicker of embers almost consumed by ashes. Fenris's handsome face faded as I woke, and I realized with an uncomfortable pang that I'd been dreaming of him. My heart clenched. Stars, why didn't I say anything to him when I left the forest?

And what could I possibly have said?

"Just keep a close eye on her. That's all I'm saying." That was Jael, speaking in low tones from somewhere behind me. I froze.

Ma sighed, and her dress rustled. "You don't honestly think she ate a death-cap?"

Jael said nothing. I bit my lip, listening.

"I mean, she does know what a deathcap is," Ma insisted.

"That's my point," Jael whispered. "What is she doing out there in the woods, all day, every day? Ma, what if she's looking for a way out?"

Ma made a strangled sort of protest, but Jael continued.

"How would any of us feel, being sold like that? And to King Nøkkyn?" His voice lowered. "You've heard the stories about what he did to his wife."

"But...we'd all starve, if she..." Ma's voice cut off.

"That's why I'm saying watch her. Keep her out of the stars-damned woods!"

There was another choked little cry. It may have been a sob, muffled in cloth.

"Egren and I will be back soon, Ma. And it's not that long until the Harvest Festival."

Another deep sigh.

"She'll be warm in the castle," Ma said. Her voice sounded pinched and thin, as though it were coming from very far away.

"That she will," Jael replied.

I closed my eyes, blocking out the dying fire that flickered and surged with the color of Fenris's hair. Deathcap mushrooms grew along the base of alder trees. They were quite innocuous looking, slender and white with delicate little caps. I'd known since I was a child to never even touch a deathcap. Half a dozen deathcaps would kill the strongest man, and just one would make you violently ill. Ill enough, I supposed, to make you stumble through the door smelling of vomit and collapse under the table.

I was awake when Jael and Egren left for the Ironwood, but I pretended to be asleep. I didn't want to meet Jael's eyes. Instead, I lay under the table, trying to ignore the contradictory demands of my parched throat and full bladder as I remembered the tattered fragments of my troubled dreams. They were filled with deathcap mushrooms, the flicker of diffused light on the mossy forest floor, and the pale blue eyes of my lover.

Only when the murmur of conversation through the open door fell silent and I heard the scrape of Ma dragging her lame leg to the herb garden, did I shake off my sleeping fur and crawl out from under the table. My head still throbbed, and my stomach felt raw and exposed. I walked to the well hunched over, wincing as my abdomen cramped, and probably looking like a crone doubled over from age. Or like someone recovering from a poisoning.

I pulled up the wooden bucket and drank deeply of the cold, clear well water before going to the outhouse. Da had built our wooden outhouse to get the first light of the morning, and Ma always planted tall, fragrant flowers along its side. It was not unpleasant, and I enjoyed the privacy its rough walls afforded.

When I stood to clean myself, the dried moss I wiped between my legs came away shiny with blood. I blinked several times as I stared at the handful of moss covered with my menstrual flow. It wasn't a surprise; the moon was new, and my menses had arrived just on time.

"This is good," I whispered to the sun-dappled walls of the outhouse.

If I'd arrived in Nøkkyn's court pregnant, I'd hang, and my family would starve. I wouldn't put it past the King to take back anything he paid for me if he discovered I'd been used before he had the chance.

So, of course this was good. I carried no child. None of the seeds Fenris planted inside me had taken root.

Still, something dark and dangerous wrapped itself around my heart, turning the emptiness of my womb into a kind of pain. I hadn't dared to hope for a new life from our furtive lovemaking. Still, late at night and in the safety of my own sleeping furs, I sometimes imagined holding a baby. Taking something of Fenris with me to Nøkkyn's castle and passing it off as the child of the King himself.

"Stupid," I muttered, shaking my head. A pregnancy would be ruinous right now, and I damn well knew it.

I spent the rest of the day hunched over in the herb garden, cutting and tying bundles to hang from our rafters during the winter. My dark mood dogged me; every time I closed my eyes, I saw Fenris jumping back as my vomit splattered across his chest.

Or I saw King Nøkkyn's pale face and cruel eyes, mouthing the words *the Reaping*.

CHAPTER THIRTEEN

"Sol, look at this!"

I rubbed my eyes and rolled over, turning toward the open door of the cabin. I'd curled up close to the fire last night, pressing a warm stone against the cramps tearing through my gut. Ma had been uncommonly gentle with me, which increased both my guilt and my black mood, and I'd spent much of the night tossing in the darkness, listening to Ma's snores as I tried not to count all the ways I'd betrayed and disappointed my family. Or the ways Nøkkyn could punish us all for my insolence.

I squinted in the morning light. Ma leaned against the doorframe with something large and round in her hands.

"What is it?" I asked.

Ma didn't respond but, even from across the room, I could see her wide smile. She limped to the table and set the thing in her hands down. I stood, pulled the sleeping fur over my shoulders, and joined her.

My mouth went dry. She'd placed a large, golden loaf of white bread on the table. Someone had taken a knife to its round, crisp surface and carved the shape of a heart.

"Well, what in the Nine Realms do you make of this?" Ma asked.

"Where did you find it?"

"In the herb garden," she said. "Just by the trail, near the basil."

Where I'd been working yesterday, I thought but did not say.

"But, who could have brought it?" she asked.

I turned away from the bread and stared at my mother. Her cheeks were flushed; the wide smile hadn't left her lips.

"I bet it was Dagnensen," I said, as casually as I could manage.

Dagnensen's wife had passed last winter, and his next spouse had been a subject of much gossipy speculation at the last Midsummer's Festival. I didn't recall Ma's name ever coming up, but it wouldn't hurt to give her a reason to smile.

"Really?" she asked.

"Well, who else could it be?" I asked feebly.

The flush across her cheeks deepened. For a moment, I could almost see the girl she had once been when she and my father begged for their freedom and started a new life together in the shadows of the Ironwood forest. I turned away from the loaf of bread. Had Fenris carved the heart here, in our herb garden, just steps away from our cabin, where I tossed and turned in my fur?

Ma ran her fingers over the heart, exactly as I had done to the rye loaf along the banks of the Lucky. Her eyes shone, and my empty stomach shifted. I shrugged out of the fur and pulled the door open, blinking at the looming darkness beneath the trees of the Ironwood.

Did you get my message? Fenris had asked me, after I discovered the first loaf.

I turned away from the forest, shaking my head.

The apples behind our house were beginning to drop, so Ma and I spent the day collecting those ripe, round globes, slicing them thin, and stringing them up to dry. The house filled with their tang, and the sight of all the apple slices dangling before the fireplace brought back an unexpectedly sharp memory of Da lifting me on his shoulders when I was a child so I could reach a dried apple slice from the ceiling, then spinning and spinning me as I shrieked with joy, the apple slice clenched in my little fists.

Our apple-strung hearth blurred as my eyes welled with tears, and I took a deep, jagged breath. Ma had insisted on splitting the bread loaf, so I'd eaten my share, although my gut still felt raw and uneasy. Now my half of the white bread sat in my stomach like a stone.

Ma's cool hand closed around my shoulder. I shrugged her off and walked away, opening the door and taking deep breaths of the cool evening air. It had been a warm day; it would have been a good day for swimming in the Lucky. Or meeting my lover along its mossy banks. Now it was over, and I'd done neither of those things.

"Sol?" Ma said from behind me.

I wiped my eyes. "I'm fine, Ma."

I heard the scrape of her leg across the floor as she backed away.

THE NEXT MORNING DAWNED cool and gray, with a light drizzle that obscured the dark edge of the Ironwood. I spent the morning bent over in the dirt, pulling garlic. After the sun rose high enough to warm the air, Ma and I sat at the table and braided the thin, green stalks into ropes we'd hang over the rafters, allowing the fat garlic bulbs to dry in the smoke of our cabin. On a sudden impulse, I'd collected handfuls of strawflowers to weave into the garlic braids. The flowers dried so beautifully, and the house always seemed like it could use those little flashes of color.

Ma sighed as she added a pink strawflower to her garlic braid. "I'd always thought I would make your bridal crown with strawflower," she said, softly.

My hand jerked. The garlic ends I'd been braiding unfurled, spilling purple and white strawflowers across the table. I met her eyes across the table; they were shiny with tears.

"You'll be all right, won't you, Sol?" she asked.

I bit my lip, unsure how to respond. My hands trembled so badly I couldn't get the garlic stems to cooperate. Frustrated, I hid them in my lap instead.

"You'll have food in the castle. And you'll be warm all winter long. Think of that, warm all winter, and you won't even have to collect the firewood!" There was a sharp, jagged edge to her voice that made me think of those dark days just after Da died, when I'd sometimes woken in the night to find her talking to him. As though he could respond.

"I'll be fine," I muttered. Anger flared in me like a wild beast thrashing at its bonds. "Maybe Nøkkyn will carve a heart in my bread," I said bitterly.

Her eyes widened, and I turned away.

"Sol, listen," Ma gasped.

I heard it. A low rumble like thunder, growing in the distance. Only it didn't stop.

"Hooves," I said.

Fear ran through me like cold water. Only one man ever rode a horse this far into the Ironwood. The taxman, who came every year to inspect our purple oak harvest.

The taxman and King Nøkkyn.

"Sol, the dress," Ma said, gesturing frantically to the chest huddled against the wall.

"But, Ma, it can't be. It's not the Reaping!"

She frowned and limped to the chest, throwing it open. I started to shake as she pulled my worn, everyday dress over my shoulders.

"Twenty days," I moaned, almost to myself. "I still have twenty days before the harvest!"

"Hush," Ma hissed.

She tugged her green dress over my head and untied my simple braid, letting my hair fall across my shoulders. That dress was cold against my skin, and its plunging neckline made me feel naked and exposed.

The hard stamp of hooves against the earth grew until it rattled the frame of our house. Men's sharp voices filled the air as Ma ran her hands through my hair, trying to arrange it over my shoulders. Her breath was hot and frantic against my ear, a hushed murmur of barely comprehensible pleas to be quiet and cooperate.

A sharp whinny pierced the air, and heavy feet hit the packed dirt of our dooryard. A moment later, the door to our cabin flew open. My body went cold. King Nøkkyn's huge frame filled the entryway to our house.

"Ugh, this place reeks of garlic." His icy voice cut through all my protests, real and imagined. "Come outside, whore. I want to see you in the light."

I turned to Ma, frantic.

"Go!" she whispered. "Sol, you must do whatever he tells you!"

She wrapped her hands around my shoulders, turning me toward the door. My stomach knotted and cramped as I stepped across the lintel, still trembling.

Two horses loomed above our herb garden, stamping and blowing in the mist. King Nøkkyn stood next to his great, black stallion, his reins clenched in his fist. Behind him, a young soldier wearing Nøkkyn's snarling bear sigil watched us with a face as impassive as stone. I wondered at the soldier's presence. Did Nøkkyn imagine I was going to put up a fight?

Nøkkyn's mouth curved into a thin, cruel smile as his small, dark eyes crawled along the exposed curve of my breasts.

"Oh, very nice," he said.

"I-I'm not ready," I stammered, staring at the churned mixture of mud and shit below his horse's hooves. "It's not the Harvest, yet."

His sharp laugh made me jump. "I'm not here to collect you, stupid little whore. I'm here to inspect the barges on the Körmt. I just wanted to test you out."

He swung up onto his horse while I frowned, trying to puzzle out the meaning of his words. "Stay here," he barked at the soldier. "And you, whore. You come with me."

King Nøkkyn turned his horse toward the Ironwood and spurred it on, leaving our dooryard at a slow trot. I took an uncertain step after him.

"You'll have to go faster than that," the soldier said, "if you don't want to make him angry."

A jolt of fear shot through me, and I started to run after Nøkkyn's black horse.

CHAPTER FOURTEEN

That damned horse was fast.

I had to run to keep up with it, even after Nøkkyn turned off the path and picked his way through the trees, seemingly at random. Fallen branches tore at the dress and snagged in my hair; my legs burned with effort. I had to hold the stupid skirt bunched in my hands as I forced my numb, exhausted legs forward, and I was only too aware of my own sweat soaking into the fabric of Ma's only fancy dress.

Despite the fire in my lungs and the slow cramp lancing my side as I ran, my mind spun with questions. What in the Nine Realms was Nøkkyn doing here? Did he want my maidenhead? My throat rasped as I sucked in breath. I'd distilled the beetroot juice, but the little clay bottle with its tight wooden stopper was still at home, nestled in a corner with the few other things I hoped to be allowed to carry to the castle. And I'd finished menstruating.

How could I fake the blood of a lost maidenhead? I bit my own lip, wondering if I could draw enough blood to smear between my legs. My foot plummeted through the pine duff, and I pitched forward. I yelped as my knee connected with a rock.

Far ahead of me, Nøkkyn's stallion pranced and whirled around. King Nøkkyn trotted back as I pulled myself to my feet, trying to brush pine needles and black dirt off my dress. He made a disapproving sort of clucking noise in the back of his throat.

"Clumsy," Nøkkyn said. "Maybe you're not worth what I'll pay for you."

I ground my teeth together to bite back my response. Nøkkyn's horse was moving again, so I doubted he would have heard it anyway. I balled my hands into fists and ran after him, trying to concentrate on finding my footing.

After we'd run for so long that I began to worry my legs would collapse under me, the great horse stopped abruptly and spun on its hooves. I staggered to a halt behind it. My chest heaved, and my legs trembled; I barely noticed King Nøkkyn swing himself down from the saddle and tie his stallion to a tree trunk.

He walked in a slow circle around me as I wiped sweat and hair from my eyes, trying to guess where we were. We'd stopped in a little clearing. Pale light filtered through the treetops, and I was glad for the light drizzle, although I suspected I'd soon be chilled. The Lucky clattered and hissed somewhere in the distance, reassuring me. If I followed the sound of that happy little river, I could always find my way home.

Nøkkyn made another circle around me, coming closer. Almost close enough to touch. I was careful not to look him in the eye, as Ma had instructed, but I watched the progress of his shiny black boots as they crushed the ground beneath their hard soles.

He grabbed my breast suddenly, without warning, and squeezed my nipple until I yelped. I glanced up at him long enough to catch his hard smile. His fingers moved up, tracing a cool line along my breastbone and around the nape of my neck.

"You smell, little whore," he said.

Shame burned through me, followed by the heat of anger. He'd made me run after his horse like a slave. I opened my mouth to speak, thought better of it, and bit my lip again. Harder this time.

His hand plunged into my hair, yanking my head back until I was forced to look at his self-satisfied smirk. He stepped closer, pressing his body against mine. I shuddered, trying to pull away. The hard leather of his breastplate scraped against the bare skin of my chest. His horse stomped the ground behind me, snorting hard.

"Shy, are we?" His breath was hot against my cheek.

He released me, and I stumbled back, still staring at the forest floor.

Nøkkyn laughed. It was sharp and unpleasant. "Whore, I own you. There's no point to shyness now."

He reached for me, his hands grasping the low neckline of the green dress. With a sickening rip, he pulled the front of the dress apart. I gasped, picturing Ma's face, remembering how she used to take that dress from the chest sometimes and just hold it on her lap, stroking it like a small, beloved animal. Nøkkyn grunted as he yanked the dress down, revealing my breasts and stomach.

"Now, that's better," he growled.

Trembling with anger, I dared to meet his eyes. "That dress was my mother's," I hissed.

Pain exploded in my cheek as my head rocked back. White stars danced across my vision. I blinked away tears as Nøkkyn cracked the knuckles on the hand he'd just used to slap me.

"I can see you'll need some training," he said. "That's good. I like the ones who need to learn their place."

Rage flooded my body. I thought of Ma and her one beautiful dress, of Jael and Egren, forced to cut the thrice-damned purple oaks deep in the Ironwood just to load the barges and line the coffers of this man. I thought of my own Da, his body horribly bent and twisted, his face already frozen a deep, violent shade of ultramarine as Jael pulled him from the darkness of the Ironwood.

"I hate you," I whispered.

Nøkkyn raised an eyebrow at me. "Is that so?"

He moved so quickly I didn't have time to react. His right fist connected with my jaw, knocking me backward, and pain blossomed across my face. I cried out as I landed, hard, on a jagged rock. My mouth filled with the sting of blood. I tried to push myself up with my hands, and pain surged through the leg that had collided with the rock.

Nøkkyn laughed, lowering himself to grab my thighs. I stopped struggling as he crawled on top of me, one leg on either side of my body. Ma's voice rang through my head in a frantic litany. *Don't ever disagree with him. Try to make him laugh.*

I closed my eyes when I felt the heat of Nøkkyn's breath on my cheek. *Don't ever tell him no,* Ma had said. His cock pressed into my stomach like a steel rod, and it was suddenly very hard for me to breathe. Somewhere behind us, his stallion gave a great, high whinny.

Nøkkyn sank his hand into my hair again, forcing my head back. He took a deep breath, running a gloved hand along my breast slowly, almost gently. I froze. My heart hammered against my ribcage as though it were trying to escape.

"Let me make one thing perfectly clear," he said, his voice calm and level. "I don't give a damn what you think."

I shivered. His hand dropped lower, pulling the shreds of Ma's dress off my stomach. My body shuddered in response.

"I'm going to fuck you now," he said, his gloved fingers sinking into the skin above my thighs. "And you're going to lay here and take it. Whore."

Panic blossomed in my chest. His touch was suddenly unbearable. My hands scraped along the ground, desperate for purchase, as I rocked my hips, trying to wiggle out from under him. His hand tightened in my hair, pulling my head back so hard tears filled my eyes.

"Do you understand?" he said.

"No," I gasped through my puffy, swollen lips. "Please, no!"

He smiled. "Good."

I saw the flash of his gloved hand from the corner of my eye.

This time, the force of his blow drove my head to the ground. My skull filled with white sparks, then faded to a dull red roar of pain. I blinked, trying to clear my vision as tree trunks wavered above me. My right eye burned, refusing to focus.

"That's good," Nøkkyn said, his voice as calm as if he'd been discussing the weather. "I like it when you scream."

He pushed himself up, and I stared at him, my body running cold with dread. He towered above me, a hard smile on his thin lips, his erection looming enormous and dark in his black pants. His long, pale fingers moved across his waist, and I realized with a slowly dawning horror that he was undoing his belt. My stomach flipped over.

I'd thought perhaps my time with King Nøkkyn wouldn't hurt because I'd already given my maidenhead to my demon, Fenris. Sometimes, when I was trying desperately to find a silver lining to the dark cloud that had eclipsed my life, I told myself I may learn to enjoy being Nøkkyn's whore. But the hard smile on those lips, and the throbbing pain from his blows, left absolutely no doubt. This was going to hurt.

Nøkkyn *wanted* it to hurt.

I pressed myself up to sitting and shoved back, away from him, scraping my skin against the rock under my thighs. Behind me, Nøkkyn's horse screamed. Despite myself, I turned toward the animal. The great stallion was straining against his tether, his white eyes huge and rolling. Foam flecked his mouth as his silver-clad hooves churned the ground below him.

"What the fuck—" Nøkkyn began.

The stallion reared, and the leather strap holding him to the tree snapped. With a great, panicked scream, the animal vanished into the Ironwood.

Nøkkyn roared in rage, and I scrambled to my feet, thanking that beautiful animal with every bit of love in my heart. I backed away from Nøkkyn and glanced into the forest, frantically wondering how far and how fast I could possibly run.

Something moved in the shadows.

Something immense, so huge it was nigh unimaginable. Nøkkyn froze as the thing stepped into sight, shattering branches as it approached.

It was black, even blacker than Nøkkyn's vanished stallion. And it was larger as well; its shoulder rose at least as high as the proud head of Nøkkyn's great steed. Its blue eyes flashed in anger as its lip curled back to reveal a row of white teeth longer and thicker than my arm.

With a blur of motion, the thing's great paw pinned Nøkkyn to the forest floor. He screamed, but I barely noticed. The enormous black wolf's pale eyes were fixed on me.

The beast lowered its jaw until it was level with my bruised and bleeding face. Its mouth opened, and it spoke in a man's voice. A voice I knew very well.

"Sol," the monster said. "You're hurt!"

I tried to force my suddenly dry mouth to form words.

"Fenris?" I gasped.

CHAPTER FIFTEEN

The great wolf didn't respond. I stared at him as his gaze moved slowly across my face. His massive eyes were the color of the winter sky at dawn. They were the exact same shade of blue as my lover's eyes.

All this time, I'd thought my secret lover had taken the name Fenris as a harmless bit of bravado, almost a joke, as if he were laughing at the dangers of the Ironwood. Now, as I stood with my puffy, split lip leaking blood into my mouth and my right eye swollen shut, another explanation for his strange name finally dawned on me. A far simpler explanation.

My lover was the Fenris-wolf. He was the monster of the Ironwood Forest.

"I-I'm—" I stammered.

Fenris's lips pulled back into a snarl, and a low, booming rumble filled the air, making my entire body shake. Fenris turned his massive head to the man pinned beneath his paw. Nøkkyn writhed under Fenris's claws like an insect.

"You hurt her!" he growled. "I'll kill you for this!"

A vision of the stony-faced guard sitting on his horse outside our cabin flashed through my mind. If King Nøkkyn didn't return, what would that soldier do to our home? To my mother?

"No!" I screamed.

Fenris turned back to me, his bright eyes wide. "Why? This man hurt you."

"This," I said, taking a deep breath, "is King Nøkkyn."

Fenris eased back slightly, allowing Nøkkyn to scramble to his feet. The king's pinched, white face was incandescent with rage.

"So? What is King Nøkkyn to you?" Fenris asked.

"She's my whore," Nøkkyn said.

Fenris's low rumbling growl filled the forest again. "Is this true?" he demanded.

My stomach curdled, and I dropped my head to my hands. There it was; everything I'd failed to tell him. The secret I'd kept from my beautiful, wild lover.

"It's true," Nøkkyn said.

Fenris ignored him. "Sol? Is it?"

I nodded miserably. "He was to collect me at the Harvest Festival."

Fenris closed his great, pale eyes, but not before I saw a flash of pain and shock burn through them.

"Do you care for this...king?" Fenris asked slowly.

"No!" I yelped, the words tumbling out of me. "No, stars, no. I hate him!"

Fenris fixed me with a cool, level gaze. "Then why are you here with him, without your clothing?"

My skin crawled as tears welled up behind my eyelids. "Because my father died. And my brothers couldn't cut enough purple oak without him. We didn't meet the quota. They had to find something to trade to King Nøkkyn, or we'd all starve."

"Oh, Sol," Fenris's eyes softened. "Why didn't you tell me? I could have helped."

I shook my head hopelessly. Yes, of course Fenris could have helped. He could have joined my brothers in the woods, he could have shared his bread—

Something silver flashed in the corner of my eye.

"Fenris!" I yelled.

King Nøkkyn darted forward, something bright glinting in his hand. He raised his fist to the massive wall of Fenris's chest and plunged both hands between Fenris's ribs. Fenris flinched, and his pelt rippled. The silver hilt of a dagger winked from deep in his black fur and then vanished as his body whirled, again crushed Nøkkyn beneath his dark claws.

"You're an irritating little thing," Fenris growled.

"So, you're the Fenris-wolf," Nøkkyn panted. "I thought you'd be bigger."

Fenris's lips curled in a snarl as they glared at each other. Then Fenris turned to me. "Sol? Are you willing to pull the king's little pin from my side?"

My mouth dry, I nodded and stepped carefully around King Nøkkyn. His eyes followed me, burning with rage and humiliation. But not fear. I swallowed hard, trying to ignore Nøkkyn's unsettling glare.

His dagger was buried in Fenris's side almost as high as my head. Blood seeped from the wound, mixing with his dark pelt. I touched the silver hilt, and Fenris shivered beneath me.

"I'm sorry," I said, through gritted teeth.

Fenris didn't respond. I wrapped my hands around the dagger's hilt and yanked hard. The effort sent a surge of sharp pain through my swollen right eye, but the dagger came clean. I landed on the pine needles, smacking myself in the chest with the bloody hilt. Then I turned to Nøkkyn, wondering how many other daggers were hidden in the folds of his dark armor.

Fenris made a sort of cough and turned back to me, his light eyes dancing. "Are you sure," he asked, "that I can't kill him?"

"It is tempting," I said as I dropped the dagger to the thick pine duff beneath my feet.

Still giving Nøkkyn a wide berth, I picked up the shreds of Ma's precious green dress from the forest floor and folded them into a tight square. Then I walked back to Fenris's side and pressed the tattered fabric against the hole left by Nøkkyn's blade. For several long minutes we were all still, my dress pressed to Fenris's wound, my hands rising and falling with his long, slow breaths as his blood slowly soaked through the green fabric, turning it black.

King Nøkkyn broke the silence. "Fenris-wolf," he said, as though we were having a casual conversation around the fireside and he wasn't being crushed beneath the claws of a legendary monster. "This woman is my whore. But, if you want her, I'm willing to trade my life for hers."

I shivered against Fenris's side.

"Her life isn't yours to give," Fenris growled.

King Nøkkyn squirmed under Fenris's toes. "Nevertheless. I'll relinquish my claim to her, and leave the two of you in peace. She could be yours, Fenris." He gave us a thin, pale smile that made my stomach churn. "Yours to take wherever your wish. Yours to do...whatever you'd like."

Fenris's sides fell still. I realized he was holding his breath, and I felt a wild surge of hope. Could it possibly be true? Would Nøkkyn let me go, just like that?

"She is quite lovely," said Nøkkyn, his dark eyes traveling my body in a way that made my skin crawl. "Those breasts, those hips. And isn't her hair just the most enchanting shade of—"

"Quiet," growled Fenris. His head swung down, almost on top of Nøkkyn.

"A woman that beautiful. She was going to be quite the prize in my collection," Nøkkyn drawled.

Fenris trembled under my hands. "King Nøkkyn," he began, his voice a low growl.

"My family!" I cried. My swollen lips made the words sound funny. "Fenris, without the money from King Nøkkyn, they'll starve!"

I stepped backward, feeling shaky. I'd almost forgotten about Ma, Jael, and Egren. Where in the Nine Realms would they be if I ran off with Fenris?

There was a shifting scrape against the earth as Fenris pulled his leg back, and then King Nøkkyn stood before us both, brushing the dirt off his elegant black pants and dark leather breastplate. He gave Fenris a level, affable smile and ignored me completely. I supposed my naked body was resistible, after all.

"I'm sure something can be arranged," Nøkkyn said.

"You will honor your commitment to Sol's family," Fenris said in a voice so low and deep I could feel it in my bones.

King Nøkkyn inclined his head slightly. "I will take care of them," he said.

"And you will relinquish all claims to Sol?" Fenris said.

Nøkkyn waved his hand dismissively. "Consider it done."

"Then you may live," Fenris said. Another low growl rippled through the clearing as his lips pulled back from his teeth. "This time."

Nøkkyn's lips twitched. It occurred to me that he looked victorious, almost as though he were struggling not to smile.

Fenris shifted against my side, his great bulk lowering. "Sol," he said. "Climb on."

With my heart in my mouth, I grabbed a handful of his thick fur and pulled myself onto his back. When he came to his feet, his back pitching and rolling like a ship in a storm, I couldn't help but scream.

His head swung back, and he fixed me with those familiar, pale eyes. "Do you really think I'd let you fall?"

I tried to smile. He gave a wild sort of cry, something between victory and joy, and we left the clearing without a backward glance. It was only much later that I realized I was completely naked, my Ma's precious green dress torn, covered with blood, and abandoned in the forest.

CHAPTER SIXTEEN

He did not let me fall, my Fenris.

We tore through the Ironwood forest like a wild beast, sliding between the trees and leaping over the rivers. Animals fled from us, deer and elk, and once even a great, lumbering bear, although he seemed tiny from my vantage point atop the wolf's back. The cool, misty air blew against my face, offering some relief from the dull throb of my injuries and, for a moment, I could imagine how free and powerful Fenris felt when he ran through the Ironwood.

He stopped along the banks of a small, bright river, which pooled at the base of several rocky hills. It may well have been the headwaters of the Lucky but, by that point, I'd completely lost my sense of direction. The bank was smooth and grassy, surrounded by an improbable collection of delicate birch trees that were somehow flourishing in the shade of the massive oaks and pines. Their pale green leaves and white bark made the forest seem lighter.

Fenris sank to his stomach on the grass. "We're here," he said, panting slightly.

I slid off and looked around. "Where is here?"

He grinned at me, showing all his monstrous, jagged teeth. "Just wait."

His enormous, dark body shuddered, and suddenly the air filled with golden sparks, as though all the fireflies in the Nine Realms were dancing around him. I gasped, hardly realizing I was taking a step back until my shoulders pressed against the papery bark of a birch tree. The light surged and swirled, completely obscuring his body, until it was almost too bright for my eyes to stand.

Then, it was gone, as suddenly as it had come. And, in the place of the great monster wolf, stood a tall, naked man, with dark auburn hair and light blue eyes. Not a demon, but not exactly a man either.

"Fenris!" I cried, flinging myself into his arms.

Demon or monster, it mattered naught to me. Fenris was my lover. He wrapped his arms around me, and we stood together, trembling, as birds called around us, and the sun slowly burned away the mist.

"My beautiful Sol," he whispered, his fingers gently tracing my bruised cheek.

I winced, then remembered Nøkkyn's cruel dagger. "Your side!" I cried, running my fingers along the ridges of his rib cage.

The wound lay halfway up his chest, between two ribs. I stepped back, staring at the crimson blood oozing down his pale skin. Of all the things I'd seen today, for some reason that cut between his ribs bothered me the most. It made everything real, somehow. I had been led into the woods by King Nøkkyn and rescued by the monster wolf, Fenris. My beautiful lover had never been a demon, and he'd given me his true name all along. His blood had stained my dress and leaked over my fingers, and now, here, my lover bore the wound of Nøkkyn's knife.

This was no dream, then. No story from Bard Sturlinsen. It was all real.

"Please, let me find some moss for that," I said.

Fenris shook his head, his eyes sparkling. "Wait here," he said.

He stepped back, disappearing into the birch grove. A bird called from deep within the forest, its voice a light and musical trill, and I had just enough time to wonder what it was. Then Fenris was back with a familiar ivory horn in his hands. My stomach lurched at the sight of it.

"Oh, no," I shook my head. "I've drunk enough mead for a lifetime, thank you."

He grinned. "Just one sip. Trust me."

My lip curled as the sweet scent of mead washed over me. "How in the Nine Realms would that help anything?"

He held out the horn, giving me a smile so joyful it almost hurt.

Oh, damn. Like I could refuse him anything. I took the horn with a snort and brought it to my mouth. The first tiny sip of mead trickled past my lips, and my body flushed with warmth. I lowered the horn; it was still almost full with glittering golden liquid.

"I'm not draining it again," I said.

Fenris' smile widened. "That's better," he said, running a finger along my lip.

I braced myself for the shock of pain that would follow. It never came. My eyes widened, and I realized my vision had cleared. I could see out of my right eye. Slowly, I raised my fingers to my own face, tracing my cheek and lips, my eye and chin.

"I'm better," I whispered. "The injuries are gone. Fenris, how?"

He kissed my cheek before responding. "It's the mead of Val-Hall," he said. "You do know what they do in Val-Hall all day, don't you?"

I frowned, trying to remember the stories I'd heard around the hearth fire. "They fight all day, to train for Ragnarök?"

"And they feast all night. But how do you think they could feast all night if they'd fought all day?"

My entire body trembled, and I looked again at the horn of mead. I'd never really believed those stories about Val-Hall; now I held their blessed mead in my hands.

"It just cures war injuries," Fenris said, almost apologetically. "Not everything, you know."

"Oh! Your side! Fenris, you have some!" I pressed the horn into his hands.

He turned, examining the scratch from Nøkkyn's dagger for the first time. "What? This tiny little thing?"

"Please," I said. I couldn't stop picturing his blood seeping through his thick, black fur, staining my mother's dress.

Fenris smiled at me, then sipped from the drinking horn. As I watched, the bloody cut from Nøkkyn's dagger closed and vanished, leaving only a thin, white scar between his ribs. I cried out despite myself and leaned forward to run my fingers along the ridges of his ribcage, feeling his warm, smooth skin shudder beneath me.

With a growl, Fenris pulled me into his arms. The drinking horn fell to the mossy ground, spilling the precious mead of Val-hall as we embraced, our tongues dancing as our bodies pressed together. By the stars, he felt so good!

I let myself forget the morning, the feel of King Nøkkyn's cold, gloved fingers on my thighs, the shudder of Fenris's enormous body as I rode him through the forest. I surrendered to the warmth of the mead, the strength of my lover's arms. My head was spinning when we pulled apart, and Fenris' breath came fast and uneven.

"Oh, Sol, I missed you," he muttered, burying his face against my neck. His breath made my body ripple with pleasure.

I moaned against him as I ran my fingers down his side, tracing the spot where Nøkkyn's knife had pierced his skin. The small raised line of scar tissue caught against my fingertips. It seemed both brave and vulnerable, a permanent reminder of how he'd risked himself to come between me and King Nøkkyn.

My heart surged in my chest. I leaned down, covering the scar with my lips. His body stiffened as I kissed his chest and his breath hissed through his lips. I knelt in front of him, hands and lips running over his taut, muscular stomach.

His manhood was stiff and thick, pointing upward at the sky and surging with need. When I wrapped my fingers around the silky skin at its base, a small drop of liquid formed on the soft head. Fenris groaned. I glanced up; his eyes were closed, and his hips rocked against my touch.

The mighty Fenris-wolf of Ironwood forest, I thought, brought low by a mere woman.

I kissed him, bringing the round tip of his cock between my lips and sucking away the pale liquid.

"Sol," he cried. "Oh, stars, Sol!"

His fingers sank into my hair, and he held my head for balance as his hips pulsed with energy. I took more of him into my mouth, caressing his head with my tongue. My lips moved up and down his length. He moaned, his fingers tightening against my skull. I ran a hand up the inside of his thigh, gently cupping the sac that hung beneath his cock. His entire body shivered in response.

Smiling, I moved lower, kissing the wrinkled skin beneath his manhood. When he groaned in pleasure, I took the sac gently in my mouth, running my fingers along the smooth tip of his manhood. I circled the sac with my tongue, feeling the two delicate eggs inside. He was trembling now, my poor Fenris.

Wrapping my arms around his thighs, I returned to his cock. I took as much as I could in my mouth, licking and sucking, devouring him the way he'd devoured me when we first met. He cried, his legs stiffening against me, his cock pulsing in my mouth.

"Sol," he panted. "Sol, I can't stop—"

I pressed my hands into his thighs, bringing him closer, deeper. And he exploded inside me, his cock throbbing as it sent his seed spilling down my throat.

I swallowed reflexively, tasting salt and a distant, subtle tang, like greens from the garden once the weather turns hot.

His body sagged against mine, and I looked up. Fenris stared at the shifting birch leaves above us, his eyes unfocused, a dazed expression on his beautiful face. As I watched, he blinked, shook his head, and turned to me.

"My beautiful Sol. You didn't need to do that."

I grinned as I let him pull me into his arms. "I wanted to."

His smile widened. For once, his face seemed open and relaxed, his forehead smooth and his eyes light. He seemed younger, somehow, as if my kiss had eased some deep, nameless fear. He kissed me, first on the cheek, then lower, to my chin, my neck, my shoulder blades, his lips moving over me softly, delicately, like moth's wings, sending shivers down my skin. Heat built in my core, slicking the inside of my thighs and tightening like a knot in my abdomen. When he pulled away, I realized I was panting.

"Sol," he whispered, gazing at me as though I were the most amazing thing in all the Nine Realms. "I never thought I'd see you here."

I broke away from his stare to glance around the clearing. It was a beautiful place, an island of bright green, pale birch bark, and dappled sunlight, hidden in the darkness of the Ironwood's thick pines. The little river gurgled softly as it curled around the massive boulders at the foot of the rocky hills beyond the birch grove.

"I never thought you'd want to come," he added, turning away from me.

"Where are we?" I asked.

He met my eyes, his face once again creased in the heavy lines of a frown. "You'll want to go home?"

"What?"

"Home. Back to that cabin you share with your mother and brothers. I can take you there."

I shivered, suddenly cool. "But...Nøkkyn said you could have me."

Fenris snorted and rocked backward. "You're not property, Sol. I can't just pick you up and run off with you, like a dairy cow."

Something dark and sharp cut through my heart, leaving my insides hollow. "I see," I whispered.

"When you're ready, I will return you." His voice sounded oddly pinched. He looked away from me toward the sparkling surface of the river.

"Is this," I began, taking a deep breath. "Is this where you live?"

He shrugged. "Not exactly."

I took a step closer to him. When I ran my fingers along the curve of his neck, he shivered and inhaled sharply.

"It's beautiful here," I said, pressing my cheek against his chest. "I don't want to leave."

He sighed, and his head sank to rest on mine. He raised his arms and wrapped them around me. I closed my eyes, listening to the rhythm of his heartbeat, breathing in his thick, rich scent.

Fenris cleared his throat. "If you—Would you want to see where I sleep?"

I smiled against the warm skin of his chest. "I'd love that."

Fenris looked almost shy as he led me from the birch grove. We walked straight toward the jagged rocks of the steep hillside, and for a second I imagined we'd climb up into the very mountains themselves. Then Fenris turned sideways, smiled apologetically, and vanished between the rocks. I yelped, and he reappeared.

"The entrance is pretty small," he said. "Sorry. You can really only get in if you go sideways."

I stepped around the mess of broken granite. There was a dark crack in the hillside, almost entirely blocked by Fenris's naked body.

"Just through here," he said, vanishing again.

Dark, narrow places have always made my heart clench. Still, I ground my teeth together and turned sideways to slip through the opening. Bare rock scraped the skin on my back and thighs, and then I was through the entrance, blinking in the gloom of a small cave.

It was barely bigger than our cabin, with jagged stone walls and a rocky floor illuminated only by the sliver of light that managed to slip in through the entrance. One stone wall was marred by the dark remnants of a small fire, and an enormous fur lay crumpled across half the floor. Several woven bags hung from the ceiling and walls, mostly empty, but a few swollen with loaves of bread. I smiled as my eyes crept around the cave a second time. It looked exactly like the hideout of a madman, or a demon.

"It's not much," Fenris said. "I've, uh, never had visitors."

I reached for the closest bag of bread, feeling its hard crust through the woven reeds. "Really? What about your friend from the Æsir?"

Fenris shook his head. "He meets me on the other side of the river. This place is...not for him." His voice faded, and I turned to him. It was too dark to be certain, but I thought he may have been blushing.

"Would you like some bread?" Fenris asked. I sensed he was eager to shift the conversation.

"No, thank you." I turned to him. "How do you fit in here? As a wolf?"

"I can't. But I've got to sleep somewhere, right?"

I didn't reply. Another implication from his words slowly sank into my consciousness. I'd been so certain Fenris had other lovers. He was so handsome, and he'd approached me with such bold confidence on the banks of the Lucky river. I'd just assumed I was one of many women he met on the cool moss beneath the trees of the Ironwood. Or perhaps I'd told myself that to assuage my guilt, as I had never once mentioned King Nøkkyn to him.

But if he'd never had visitors— If I was the only woman who had ever seen the inside of his cave, the place where the mighty Fenris-wolf slept—

"You saved me," I whispered. My voice sounded as rough as the walls of stone surrounding us. "From King Nøkkyn. You rescued me, like in one of Bard Sturlinsen's stories."

Fenris shook his head. His eyes were wide and liquid. "I'm no hero."

"But, you saved me from the wicked king."

"No." Fenris shifted on his feet and turned away. "Sol, I— I would have let you go with Nøkkyn. If you'd said that's what you wanted. But—"

He pulled a sharp breath over his lips. It was almost a gasp of pain.

"It would have felt like dying." Fenris rocked back and forth, then sank his hands into his hair. "All those stories, those Sturlinsen fantasies. They make it sound like falling in love is something magical. But, stars, Sol. For me, it's been torture. And, when you leave, it's going to kill me."

He glanced up again, just long enough for the thin light streaming through the cave's entrance to dance along the tears pooled in his pale eyes. Then he turned his back to me and rocked forward, as if his body ached to run.

"Fenris."

He stiffened as I said his name. It was a small enough cave I only had to extend my arm to touch him, and take a single step to wrap my arms around him. His heart hammered against his chest as though he'd just run the length of the

Ironwood, and the words he'd just spoken seemed to hang in the air between us.

Love.

I'd never thought to use that word with Fenris, my mad, handsome lover from the Ironwood. Since the day King Nøkkyn grabbed my breast through the soft fabric of Ma's green dress and declared my worth equal to twenty cords of purple oak, I'd tried not to think of love at all. Love belonged to girls like Maddie Liefsen who wore ribbons in their hair and had shoes to protect their delicate toes from the mud.

But now everything had changed. Fenris, the monster of the Ironwood, had rescued me. He'd stolen me away from the wicked king and had taken me to his secret home deep in the darkness of the Ironwood.

I was free.

And, yes, by the Realms! There was a word for this feeling, for the ache in my chest whenever I imagined my life without Fenris, for the sense that I would die without him, that I was only truly alive when the two of us were together. Since we'd first come together on the mossy banks of the Lucky River, that moment when I decided I wanted him and not King Nøkkyn, Fenris had filled my waking moments and chased my dreams. He'd brought me more joy than I'd thought the Nine Realms could hold.

That was what people meant when they said love.

"I don't want to leave," I said. "I love you, too."

The words felt so right rising from my lips. As if my love for him had been woven into the fabric of the Nine Realms from the very beginning, lying dormant for the long aeons before my birth, just waiting for me to turn toward Fenris and speak the truth my heart had always known.

Slowly, with every muscle of his body taut, Fenris turned to face me. A single tear streaked down his cheek, cutting a gleaming path along the curve of his cheekbones. I wiped it away with my fingertip.

"Fenris, I—"

His lips crashed against mine, stopping any further conversation. He kissed me with a sudden, desperate ferocity, as if he thought I might change my mind, decide to leave the cave and abandon him.

The thought made me shudder. I reached for him, wrapping my arms around his chest and sinking my hands into his thick hair. I met his storm of kisses with my own fierce need, and all my wild joy at my rescue. We sank together to the stack of furs lining the cave's floor, our arms and legs entangled, our bodies already slick with sweat and anticipation.

I opened for him with no hesitation, and no words. Fenris gasped as he slid inside me, filling me, completing me. Then his mouth met mine again, and our lips and tongues danced even as our bodies came together. When we drew breath, we drew it as one.

This is freedom, I thought, as his body rippled above me, his pleasure echoing and heightening mine.

This is love.

Fenris and Sol's Story Continues in The Monster's Wife

I followed the stream back to the cave, the latent flicker of my arousal growing with every step as I pictured the smooth lines of Fenris's body, the curve of his neck meeting his shoulder, the spread of his chest beneath my fingertips.

The sound of whistling reached me, and I paused. Odd. I'd never heard Fenris whistle before. He must not be wearing the wolf's shape, then. I glanced at the little stream and grinned. I could surprise him.

From the sound of his cheerful whistle, Fenris was almost in sight. I walked to the water and dipped my toes in. A twig snapped in the forest, and I lowered myself into the stream, shivering. My hair swirled in the water as I pressed my body against the bank and crawled downstream a pace or two, until I reached a spot where a great mass of roots nearly hid the bank from view. The stream was almost cold enough to take my breath away, but I hunched down motionless beneath the tangle of roots, imagining Fenris's face when I burst from the river, my nipples taut, my skin glistening and wet.

I waited until the sound of his footfalls was almost on top of me. Then I pressed my toes into the sandy stream bed and leapt from the water.

"Surprise!" I cried.

The man in front of me gasped and stumbled backward. He was not Fenris.

I screamed.

Pre-order The Monster's Wife, the second book in The Fenris Series, here[1]!

---

1. *https://www.amazon.com/dp/B07M85NN6W/ref=sr_1_10?ie=UTF8&qid=1547498728&sr=8-10&key-words=samantha+macleod*

Thank You!

Thank you so much for your support of independent authors!

Without encouragement from readers like you, I wouldn't be writing. It takes both of us to make the magic happen.

Now that you've finished *The Monster's Lover,* please do consider leaving a review. Reviews make or break the careers of independent authors like me, and I promise, I really do read every single one.

You can leave a review on Goodreads[1] or the retailer of your choosing.

---

1. https://www.goodreads.com/book/show/43311545-the-monster-s-lover

Who is Týr?

Join Samantha MacLeod's mailing list and get a **free** copy of ***Tempting Fenris Wolf***, a short story featuring Týr and Fenris.

<u>Click here to sign up!</u>[1]

---

1. https://www.subscribepage.com/t0v9u6

More from Samantha MacLeod

The Loki Series
    The Trickster's Lover[1]
Honeymoon[2]
The Wolf's Lover[3]
The Trickster's Song[4]
The Loki Series Box Set[5]

THE FENRIS SERIES
    The Monster's Lover
    The Monster's Wife[6] (coming Feb. 2019)
    The Monster and the Prisoner (coming March 2019)
    The Monster Chained (coming May 2019)
    The Monster Freed (coming July 2019)

EROTIC SHORT STORIES

---

1.   *https://www.amazon.com/Tricksters-Lover-Samantha-MacLeod/dp/0997689811*

2.   *https://www.amazon.com/Honeymoon-Steamy-Novella-Samantha-MacLeod-ebook/dp/B01M7ZW-SOM/ref=asap_bc?ie=UTF8*

3.   *https://www.amazon.com/Wolfs-Lover-Urban-Fantasy-Romance-ebook/dp/B078VNWKT3*

4.   *https://www.amazon.com/Tricksters-Song-Loki-Book-ebook/dp/B07GL3HS7T/ref=sr_1_9?ie=UTF8&qid=1534585888&sr=8-9&keywords=samantha+macleod*

5.   *https://www.amazon.com/Loki-Box-Set-Samantha-MacLeod-ebook/dp/B07KCJY64R/ref=sr_1_12?ie=UTF8&qid=1541857047&sr=8-12&keywords=samantha+macleod*

6.   *https://www.amazon.com/dp/B07M85NN6W/ref=sr_1_10?ie=UTF8&qid=1547498728&sr=8-10&keywords=samantha+macleod*

Persephone Remembers the Pomegranates[7] (free!)
Claiming Thor's Hammer[8]
Winning Freyja's Cloak[9]
Legends & Lovers[10] (short story collection)

URBAN FANTASY & FANTASY Romance
Hel's Lover[11] (fantasy romance inspired by Norse myth)
The Night Watch[12] (M/M/M/F fantasy romance)

Join Samantha's Review Team and be the first to see new releases[13]!

---

7.   https://www.amazon.com/Persephone-Remembers-Pomegranates-Romance-Inspired-ebook/dp/B01MY43NP7/ref=asap_bc?ie=UTF8

8.   https://www.amazon.com/Claiming-Thors-Hammer-Erotic-Adventure-ebook/dp/B076X4M31W

9.   https://www.amazon.com/Winning-Freyjas-Cloak-Erotic-Fantasy-ebook/dp/B07DX9G8D9/ref=sr_1_9?s=books&ie=UTF8&qid=1529694124&sr=1-9

10.   https://www.amazon.com/Legends-Lovers-stories-inspired-fantasy-ebook/dp/B07KX1F2Y1/ref=sr_1_11?ie=UTF8&qid=1543414107&sr=8-11&keywords=samantha+macleod

11.   https://www.amazon.com/Death-Beauty-Fantasy-Inspired-Mythology-ebook/dp/B071L88ZH7/ref=asap_bc?ie=UTF8

12.   https://www.amazon.com/Night-Watch-Samantha-MacLeod-ebook/dp/B077SZBNFW/ref=sr_1_3?s=digital-text&ie=UTF8&qid=1515328587&sr=1-3

13. https://www.subscribepage.com/v5c4v3

Acknowledgements

Thank you, first and foremost, to my very patient husband. You'll always be my alpha reader, honey.

Ravenborn Covers designed this fabulous cover and the rest of the covers in this series. Anika, you do amazing work!

I was fortunate enough to work with two very talented and patient editors who gave invaluable advice and feedback. Kate of BFF Editing and Christine of Round Table Author Services were both incredibly helpful and very generous. I highly recommend both of them.

Thank you, as always, to the wonderful community of writers I've found who manage to blend high literature and erotica. Here's a shout out to Janine Ashbless, Liz Meldon, Bronwyn Green, Mira Stanley, Torrance Sene, and many others who have encouraged me to keep writing. If you're looking for your next read, you can't go wrong with one of those fabulous authors.

Thanks to my family for your patience while I burn dinners, ignore the laundry, refuse to return your phone calls, and generally let my life unravel for yet another smut book.

And, finally, thank **you**. Without readers, this story wouldn't exist.